ISBN 0 86112 648 3
This edition © Brimax Books Ltd 1990
All rights reserved
Published by Brimax Books, Newmarket, England
Second printing 1991
Printed in Spain by Graficromo, S.A., Cordoba

PETER PAN

By

J. M. BARRIE

Adapted by Peter Oliver

Illustrated by ERIC KINCAID

BRIMAX BOOKS • NEWMARKET • ENGLAND

Introduction

James Barrie's masterpiece about Peter Pan, Wendy and
the Lost Boys on the island of Neverland has thrilled
and enchanted generations of children.

There never was a more mischievous or cockier lad than
Peter, the boy who never grew up. His story is an
exciting voyage into the vivid make-believe world of
every child's imagination.

Grown-ups have long forgotten where Neverland is. But
to the Darling children, Wendy, John and Michael – and
every young reader – its dangers and adventures are
all too real.

The Darling Family, of course, lived at No 14.
They were a very ordinary family, even though
Mr and Mrs Darling had a large dog called Nana to
nurse the children.

Yet Nana was so clever. It was she who sensed danger
the night Peter Pan flew into the children's bedroom,
taught them how to fly and tempted them away to
Neverland.

There on the island lived the sad Lost Boys, who had
never had a mother. It was also home to the Redskins,
strange mermaids, a jealous fairy called Tinker Bell,
a huge crocodile and Peter Pan's sworn enemy, the
terrifying pirate, Captain Hook.

When Captain Hook captures Wendy and the children, they
all seem doomed to walk the plank of the Jolly Roger. Will
Mr and Mrs Darling ever see their children again?

Acclaimed children's book illustrator Eric Kincaid
has perfectly captured the magic of James Barrie's
fantasy in this new adaptation for today's readers.

Contents

CHAPTER ONE

Peter Pan's Arrival

All children, except one strange little boy, grow up one day. Wendy knew she would have to grow up when she was just two years old. She was playing in the garden and picked a flower for her mother. Mrs Darling saw her daughter running towards her and smiled because Wendy looked so enchanting. 'Oh, why can't you remain like this for ever!' she cried.

Wendy understood then that she wouldn't always be two. It was the beginning of the end, really. Some day, she too would be a grown-up.

Mrs Darling was a perfect mother with a kind face and the prettiest mouth you ever saw. It was full of kisses. Mrs Darling loved to kiss her children, yet there always seemed to be one special kiss which Wendy could never get. There it was, plain enough, on the right-hand corner of Mrs Darling's mouth. One day someone would steal that kiss.

When Mrs Darling was just a girl herself, all the boys fell in love with her. They ran to ask her to marry them. But clever Mr Darling beat them all because he took a taxi and got there first. So Mrs Darling married George. But even he could not get that special kiss.

Mr and Mrs Darling lived in a tree-lined street, and their house was No 14. They had three children. Wendy was the first to be

born, followed soon after by John and then Michael. The Darlings adored them all.

Mr Darling worked in the city. No one was quite sure what he did, but he knew about stocks and shares, and those sorts of things. Each morning he went off to work, looking very important with his brief case and umbrella. One thing about Mr Darling was that he liked to keep up with his neighbours. Next door they had a nanny for the children, so the Darlings got one, too.

But as the family was so poor, the nanny the Darlings found was a prim Newfoundland dog called Nana. She had not belonged to anyone in particular before. The Darlings first spotted her in London's Kensington Gardens, where Nana was forever peeping into prams to make sure the babies were being looked after properly.

Nana might have been a rather unusual nanny, but she was indeed a treasure. She was so good with the children at bath-time, and up at any moment of the night if the children made the slightest cry. She slept in a kennel in the nursery.

Nana was so clever. She always knew if a child's cough was something which needed medicine. She believed in old-fashioned remedies like rhubarb leaf, and hated all the new-fangled talk of germs.

You should have seen Nana taking the children to school. She walked quietly by their side when they were well-behaved, or butted them in the back if they were naughty. When John was playing football she never forgot his sweater, and she usually carried an umbrella in her mouth in case of rain.

The children went to Miss Fulsom's Kindergarten. In the afternoon Nana would join the other nannies waiting for the children to finish school. They sat on benches while Nana lay on the floor, but that was the only difference. The nannies took no notice of Nana because they thought her very inferior. Nana in turn ignored them because of their silly gossip.

Everyone in the family loved Nana, except for Mr Darling. He wondered uneasily if the neighbours talked about them, for having such a strange nanny. After all, he did have his position in the city to consider. Mr Darling also suspected that Nana did not admire him as much as he thought she should.

But all in all the Darlings were a happy family. In fact there never was a happier family until the coming of Peter Pan.

*   *   *

I don't know whether you have ever seen a map of a person's mind. Doctors can sometimes draw maps of other parts of you, but they could never draw a map of a child's mind. It's like a chest of drawers, full of strange bits and pieces; childish secrets, memories of your first day at school and thoughts about when mother is going to serve your favourite chocolate pudding for tea.

Hidden in a corner of all that jumble is the make-believe world of Neverland. It has a special place in every child's mind. Neverland is almost always an island and it has coral reefs and boats, redskins, and lonely hideouts. It's a place where gnomes live and caves have rivers running through them. Somewhere on the island there is aways an old lady with a crooked nose.

Of course, the Neverlands vary a lot in each child's mind. John's Neverland, for instance, had a lagoon with flamingoes flying over it, while Michael, who was very small, had a flamingo with lagoons flying over it. In John's Neverland he lived in an upturned boat, Michael in a wigwam and Wendy in a house of leaves sewn together. John had no friends, Michael had friends at night and Wendy had a pet wolf which had been left by its mother.

On the magical shores of Neverland children are forever beaching their boats to play. We have all been there and we can still hear the sound of the surf breaking on the island shore. But some of us will never land there again because we are grown up now.

The Neverland is not a frightening place by day when children are at play. But just before you go to sleep, it can become all too real. That's why some mothers put night-lights by the bedside to stop children becoming frightened.

Mrs Darling often tried to look into her children's minds last thing at night, hoping to find out what they were thinking. Sometimes she discovered things in their heads which she could not understand. Quite the most baffling of these was the word Peter. She knew of no Peter and yet he was there in John and Michael's minds, while the name was written all over Wendy's mind.

'Who is he, my pet?' asked Mrs Darling, kneeling beside Wendy's bed.

'He is Peter Pan, mother,' answered Wendy.

Mrs Darling, who had her own Neverland as a child, recalled vague memories of a Peter Pan who was said to live with the fairies. She remembered odd stories about him. Wasn't he the

boy who, when children died, went part of the way with them so they wouldn't be frightened? She had believed in Peter Pan then, but now she was grown up, married and far too sensible. She doubted whether there was any such person. 'Besides,' she said to Wendy, 'he would be grown up by now.'

'Oh, he isn't grown up,' said Wendy, who by now was nearly ten years old. 'He is the same size as me.' She didn't know how she knew. She just knew.

Later, Mrs Darling mentioned Peter Pan to her husband. But he pooh-poohed the whole idea. 'Mark my words,' he said, 'it's some nonsense Nana has been putting into their heads. It's just the sort of idea a dog would have. Leave it alone and the children will soon forget it.'

But it did not blow over and soon the troublesome boy gave Mrs Darling quite a shock. It was Wendy who gave her the strange news. Some leaves from a very strange tree had been found on the nursery floor, leaves which certainly hadn't been there when the children went to bed.

'I do believe it is Peter again,' said Wendy.

'Whatever do you mean, Wendy?' asked her mother.

'The leaves must have stuck to his shoes,' said Wendy, who was a very tidy girl. 'It was naughty of him not to wipe his feet before he came in.'

Wendy explained in a quite matter-of-fact way that she thought Peter Pan sometimes came into the nursery at night and sat at the foot of her bed, playing music on his pipes. Unfortunately she never woke, so she couldn't explain to her mother how she knew. She just knew.

'What nonsense you talk, precious,' said Mrs Darling. 'No one can get into the house without knocking.'

'I think he comes in by the window,' said Wendy.

'My love, the nursery is three floors up.'

'Weren't the leaves at the foot of the window, mother?' said Wendy proudly.

Mrs Darling did not know what to think. Later she examined the leaves closely. They were skeleton leaves and she was sure they did not come from any tree that grew in England. Had some strange boy been in the room? She searched for any strange footprints and even rattled the poker up the chimney to make sure he wasn't hiding there. She found nothing. 'Wendy must be dreaming,' said Mrs Darling.

But Wendy had not been dreaming, as the very next night showed. It was the night on which the extraordinary adventures of the children began. It was Nana's night off and the children were all in bed. Mrs Darling sang to them and, one by one, they let go of her hand and slid away into the land of sleep.

They all looked so cosy in bed and Mrs Darling forgot her fears as she settled into a chair to do some sewing. The nursery was dimly lit by the three night-lights and the fire was warm. Very soon she fell asleep.

While Mrs Darling slept, she had a dream. She dreamt that the Neverland had come too near and that a strange boy had appeared. He did not alarm her. But in the dream he had drawn aside the hazy curtain which always hides Neverland. Mrs Darling saw Wendy, John and Michael peeping through the gap.

The dream itself might have meant nothing, but while she was dreaming the window of the nursery blew open and a boy dropped down onto the floor. He was accompanied by a strange tiny light, no bigger than your fist. It darted around the room like a living thing, and it must have been this light which woke Mrs Darling.

She jumped up with a cry, and saw the boy. Somehow she knew at once that he was Peter Pan. He was a lovely boy, dressed in skeleton leaves. But the most delightful thing about him was that he still had all his baby teeth.

He saw Mrs Darling was a grown-up and gnashed his pearly little teeth at her.

CHAPTER TWO

Peter Pan's Shadow

Mrs Darling screamed. Hardly had the sound left her mouth than Nana returned from her evening out and ran into the nursery. She growled and sprang at the boy, who escaped through the window. Again Mrs Darling screamed, but this time she was worried what had happened to the boy. She ran down to the street to look for his little body which she expected would be lying on the ground. But it was not there. She looked up and in the black night she could see nothing but a shooting star.

She returned to the nursery to find Nana with something in her mouth. It was the boy's shadow. As he leapt through the window, Nana had closed it, too late to catch the boy, but quickly enough to stop his shadow escaping. Slam went the window and snapped the shadow off.

Mrs Darling examined the shadow carefully, but really it was quite a normal sort of shadow.

Nana had no doubt what was the best thing to do with the shadow. She hung it out at the window, sure that the boy would return for it later. But Mrs Darling could not leave it hanging there. It looked like she had hung the washing out and what would the neighbours think? She rolled up the shadow and put it away carefully in a drawer. There it would stay until she could find a good time to tell Mr Darling all about it.

Her chance came a week later, on a Friday, a never-to-be-forgotten Friday. It was the day that Mr and Mrs Darling had been invited to dine at No. 27. As evening came and they dressed for the dinner, everything was as normal in the Darling household. Nana put the water on for Michael's bath and was carrying him on her back to the bathroom.

'I won't have a bath. I won't go to bed,' shouted Michael in protest. 'It isn't six o'clock yet. I shan't love you any more Nana if you make me. I won't be bathed. I won't!'

Then Mrs Darling came in wearing her white evening gown. She had dressed early because Wendy loved to see her in the gown. She was also wearing Wendy's bracelet on her arm. Wendy was so proud to lend the bracelet to her mother.

Mrs Darling found Wendy and John playing a favourite game, mothers and fathers, pretending that they were Mr and Mrs Darling and Wendy had just been born. 'I am happy to tell you, Mrs Darling, that you are now a mother,' said John.

Wendy danced with joy, just as Mrs Darling must have done when Wendy was really born. Wendy and John had just got to the part of the game where John was born when Michael returned from his bath and said he wanted to be born as well. But John replied heartlessly: 'We don't want any more children.'

Michael nearly cried. 'Nobody wants me,' he said.

Mrs Darling, looking on, could not bear it. 'I do want another child,' she said. 'I so want a third child.'

'Boy or girl?' asked Michael, not too hopefully.

'Oh a boy,' said Mrs Darling. 'Certainly a little boy just like you.'

Michael leapt into his mother's arms in delight and was still locked in embrace when Mr Darling rushed in. In his hand was a tie and he was looking furious. 'What's the matter, dear?' asked Mrs Darling.

'Matter?' he yelled. 'This tie is driving me mad. This tie will not tie. Not round my neck! Round the bedpost! Oh yes, twenty times I have tied it round the bedpost. But round my neck? Oh, no.'

Mrs Darling smiled to herself at the sight of her husband in such a tantrum. He had always had a short temper, 'I warn you, mother,' he stormed, 'unless this tie is round my neck soon, we won't go out to dinner tonight. And if I don't go out to dinner tonight, I will never go to my office again. And if I don't go to the office, you and I will starve, and our children will be flung out on the streets.'

'Come dear,' said Mrs Darling, 'let me try.'

It was done in a trice and Mr Darling forgot his rage at once, and was soon dancing round the room with Michael on his back. All the children joined in. Nana, hearing all the fuss, wandered in, too. Unluckily she brushed against Mr Darling's new trousers, covering them with her hairs. He was so angry and once more said how stupid it was to have a dog for a nanny.

'Nana is a treasure,' said Mrs Darling, brushing off the hairs.

'I think she looks on the children as puppies,' snapped Mr Darling.

'Oh, no, dear,' said Mrs Darling. 'I'm sure she knows they are different.'

Just then Mrs Darling had a thought. Perhaps now was the time to tell her husband about the boy and his shadow. So she did. He laughed at first, but became very thoughtful when she showed him the shadow.

'It is nobody I know,' he said, examining it carefully, 'but he does look like a scoundrel.'

Nana returned with some cough medicine for Michael. She poured it into a spoon, but Michael couldn't bear to drink the dreadful stuff. 'I won't take it,' Michael cried naughtily. 'Won't! Won't!'

'Be a man,' said Mr Darling. 'When I was your age I took medicine without a murmur.'

Wendy joined the conversation. 'Father has to take medicine even now, and it's much nastier than Michael's, isn't it, father?'

'Ever so much nastier,' said Mr Darling. 'I would take mine now if I hadn't lost the bottle.'

He had not exactly lost his medicine. In the dead of the night he had climbed to the top of the wardrobe to hide it. But Liza, the Darling's faithful servant, had found it and put it back beside Mr Darling's bed.

'I know where the medicine is,' cried Wendy, always glad to be helpful. 'I'll bring it.' She ran off before he could stop her and Mr Darling's spirits sank. It was such beastly medicine.

Wendy returned with the medicine in a glass. Mr Darling frowned. 'Michael, you take yours first,' he mumbled.

'No father, you first,' said Michael, who was suspicious by nature.

'I shall be sick, you know,' said Mr Darling. 'Besides, there's more in my glass than there is on your spoon. It isn't fair.'

'I thought you said you could easily take your medicine,' said Wendy.

'Father, I'm waiting,' said Michael.

'It's all very well to say you are waiting,' said Mr Darling. 'So am I waiting.'

'Father's a cowardy custard.'

'So are you a cowardy custard.'

'I'm not frightened,' said Mr Darling.

'Neither am I frightened,' said Michael.

'Well, then, take your medicine.'

'Well, then, you take yours.'

Wendy came up with the answer. 'Why don't you both take it at the same time?'

'Certainly,' said Mr Darling. 'Are you ready, Michael?'

Wendy gave the words; one, two, three. Michael took his medicine, but Mr Darling slipped his behind his back. There was a yell of rage from Michael.

'Stop that row, Michael,' said Mr Darling. 'I meant to take mine, but . . . I think I've taken mine already today.'

The children all gave their father shaming looks and he thought he would try to make a joke out of the whole thing. 'I shall pour my medicine into Nana's bowl and she can drink it. She'll think it's milk.'

The children did not share their father's sense of humour and there were no smiles as he poured the medicine into the bowl. He patted Nana when she returned from cleaning up the bathroom. 'Good dog,' he said, patting Nana's head. 'Look, there's some milk in your bowl.'

Nana wagged her tail, ran to the bowl and began lapping the medicine. She gave Mr Darling such a look. It wasn't an angry stare, just a very sad one. Then she crept into her kennel. Wendy immediately went over and gave Nana a big cuddle.

Mr Darling knew he should not have done it, but he could not give in. 'It was only a joke,' he said, growing angry again. 'I will not allow that dog to lord it in my nursery for an hour longer,' he said. 'The proper place for that dog is in the yard, and there it will go to be tied up this instant.'

The children wept and Nana ran to Mr Darling, but he waved her away. Mrs Darling did her best. 'Remember what I told you about the boy,' she said. 'Remember how Nana chased him away. You must not punish Nana.'

Mr Darling would not listen because he was determined to show that he was the master of the house. He seized Nana and dragged her from the nursery. He was ashamed of himself but he still did it. When he had tied Nana to a chain in the backyard,

he went and sat in the passage feeling rather sad and guilty at what he had done.

Meanwhile Mrs Darling put the children to bed and lit their night-lights. They could all hear Nana barking and John whispered: 'It's because she has been tied up.'

Wendy was wiser. 'That is not Nana's unhappy bark,' she said. 'That is her bark when she smells danger.'

'Danger!' started Mrs Darling. 'Are you sure?'

'Oh yes,' said Wendy.

Mrs Darling shivered a little and went to the window. It was securely shut. She looked out and saw that the night sky was peppered with stars. It was as if the stars were crowding round the house to see what was happening inside. But Mrs Darling did not notice that, nor that one or two of the smaller stars winked at her. Yet she felt frightened. 'Oh, how I wish that I wasn't going out to dinner tonight,' she said.

Even Michael, already half asleep, knew she was worried. 'Can anything harm us after the night-lights are lit?' he asked.

'Nothing, precious,' she said. 'Night-lights are the eyes a mother leaves behind to guard her children.'

She sang lullabies to the children until they were all asleep and then she crept from the room.

* * *

No. 27 was only a few yards further up the street. Mr and Mrs Darling closed the door of No. 14 and walked out into the silent street which had been covered by a slight fall of snow. They were the only people to be seen and all the stars were watching. That's all stars can do. They cannot take an active part in anything. It is punishment put on them for something they did so long ago that no star remembers what it was.

The stars are not really friendly to Peter because he has a mischievous way of creeping up on them and trying to blow out their lights. But they are so fond of fun that they were on his side on this special night and anxious to get the grown-ups out of the way. So as soon as Mr and Mrs Darling entered No. 27 and the door closed, there was a sudden flurry of activity in the heavens.

The smallest of all the stars screamed out: 'Now, Peter!'

CHAPTER THREE

Come Away, Come Away

After Mr and Mrs Darling left the house, the night-lights by the beds of the three children continued to burn brightly for a moment. Then, one by one, they blinked, yawned and went out. There was another light in the room now, a thousand times brighter than the night-lights.

In no time at all the light had flashed around the room, looking in all the drawers for Peter's shadow, searching in the wardrobe and turning every pocket inside out. It was not really a light because when it came to rest you saw it was a fairy, no taller than the length of a hand. It was a girl called Tinker Bell and she was perfectly dressed in a skeleton leaf gown.

A moment after the fairy's arrival, the window was blown open by the breathing of the little stars and Peter Pan dropped in. He had carried Tinker Bell part of the way and his hands were still covered in fairy dust.

'Tinker Bell,' he called out softly, after making sure that the children were asleep. 'Tink, where are you?'

Tinker Bell was busily playing in a jug. It was great fun because she had never been in a jug before.

'Oh, come out of that jug,' said Peter. 'Have you found out where they put my shadow?'

A tinkle of golden bells answered him. It was fairy language and Peter understood it. Tink said that the shadow was in the big box. She meant the chest of drawers, but Peter guessed what she was saying. He jumped at them, scattering their contents on the floor. In a moment he found his shadow and shut the drawer. He was so happy again that he forgot that he had shut up Tinker Bell inside.

If Peter ever thought at all, and I don't think he ever did, he would have imagined that he and his shadow would have joined up quite naturally again. But they did not. He tried to stick it on with soap from the bathroom, but that also failed. Peter thought he would never be able to join his shadow ever again. He sat on the floor and cried.

His sobs woke Wendy and she sat up in bed. She was not alarmed to see a stranger on the floor. She was indeed quite interested. 'Boy,' she said politely. 'Why are you crying?'

Peter could also be very polite. He stood up and bowed to Wendy quite beautifully. She was delighted and bowed in return. 'What's your name?' Peter asked.

'Wendy Moira Angela Darling. What's yours?'

'Peter Pan.'

Wendy had already guessed that this must be Peter Pan. 'Where do you live?' she asked.

'Second to the right,' said Peter, 'and straight on till morning.'

'What a funny address.'

'No it isn't,' he said.

Wendy did not want to be rude. 'Sorry,' she said. 'I mean, is that the address they put on your letters?'

'Don't get letters,' said Peter.

'But surely your mother does?'

'Don't have a mother,' he said. Not only did Peter not have a mother, he had no wish to have one. He thought them very silly things.

'Oh, Peter,' said Wendy sadly, getting out of bed to comfort him. 'No wonder you were crying.'

'I wasn't crying about mothers,' said Peter rather indignantly. 'I was crying because I can't get my shadow to stick on. Besides I wasn't crying.'

And if you believe Peter Pan, and some people don't, he would always tell you he never cried or slept.

Wendy saw the shadow on the floor and felt terribly sorry for Peter. 'How awful,' she said, but she could not help smiling when she saw how he had tried to stick it on with soap. How

Wendy saw the shadow on the floor
and felt terribly sorry for Peter.

exactly like a boy! 'I know what to do. I'll sew it on,' she said.

'What's sew?' asked Peter.

'You're dreadfully ignorant,' said Wendy.

'No, I'm not'.

'Never mind. I will sew it on for you, my little man,' she said, although he was as tall as herself. 'It might hurt a little.'

'Oh, I shan't cry,' said Peter.

Wendy got out her sewing bag and, as Peter clenched his teeth, she sewed the shadow onto his foot. He was delighted and jumped around in glee, quickly forgetting who had helped him regain his shadow. 'How clever I am,' he crowed. 'Oh, the cleverness of me.'

There never was a more cockier boy and Wendy had never heard such a cocky crow.

'I suppose I did nothing?' said Wendy.

'You did a little,' Peter said, and continued to dance.

'In that case,' she said a little haughtily, 'if you have no more use for me, I will go back to bed.'

Wendy got back into bed and covered her head with the blankets. Peter tried to get her to look up by pretending he was going, and when that failed, he tapped her gently with his foot. 'Wendy,' he said. 'I can't help it, I can't help crowing when I'm pleased with myself.'

Wendy still wouldn't look up, but she was listening closely. 'Wendy,' he continued with the angelic voice he put on for special occasions. 'Wendy, one girl is more use than twenty boys.'

Peter's charm worked. She peeped out from beneath her bedclothes. 'Do you really think so?'

'Yes, I do.'

'In that case I think you are very sweet,' she declared, 'and I'll get up again.'

She sat with him on the side of the bed and said she would give him a kiss if he liked. But Peter did not know what she meant, and he held out his hand to receive the kiss. 'Surely you know what a kiss is?' she said.

'I shall know when you give it to me,' he replied stiffly, holding out his hand.

Wendy did not want to hurt Peter's feelings over not knowing what a kiss was. So she gave him a thimble instead.

'Now,' said Peter, 'Shall I give you a kiss?'

'If you please,' said Wendy, sad that Peter had clearly never been kissed.

She did not know whether to expect a kiss or not, so she put her cheek closer to him, but he merely took an acorn button from his coat and put it into her hand. She said that she would wear his kiss on the chain round her neck. It was lucky that she did put it on that chain, because later on it would save her life.

Wendy asked Peter how old he was, but he did not know. 'I think I am quite young,' he said. 'I ran away the day I was born.'

Wendy was surprised at his words and told him to sit closer. 'It was because I heard father and mother talking,' he explained in a low voice. 'They were talking about what I was to be when I became a man. I don't ever want to be a man. I want always to be a little boy and have fun. So I ran away to Kensington Gardens and lived a long time among the fairies.'

Wendy was fascinated and asked so many questions about the fairies. Her interest quite surprised Peter because he thought the subject of fairies rather boring. In fact he found them so troublesome that sometimes he had to give them a hiding. Still he liked them on the whole and he told Wendy how the fairies began.

'You see Wendy, when the first baby laughed for the very first time, its laugh broke into a thousand pieces, and they all went skipping about, and that was the beginning of the fairies.'

Wendy listened wide-eyed as he continued. 'You know, there ought to be a fairy for every boy and girl.'

'Ought to be?' said Wendy. 'Isn't there?'

'No. You see, children know such a lot these days, they soon don't believe in fairies. And every time a child says "I don't believe in fairies", there is a fairy somewhere that falls down dead.'

Peter Pan thought he had said enough about fairies and began to wonder where Tinker Bell was. 'I can't think where she has gone to,' he said.

He got off the bed and called Tink by name. Wendy's heart fluttered with excitement. 'Peter,' she cried, clutching his arm. 'You don't mean to tell me there is a fairy in this room!'

'She was here just now,' said Peter. 'You don't hear her, do you?'

'The only sound I can hear,' said Wendy, 'is like a tinkle of bells.'

'That's Tink,' said Peter. 'That's fairy language. I think I can hear her, too.'

The sound came from the chest of drawers and Peter began to

smile. No one could ever look quite so merry as Peter and he had the loveliest of gurgles for a laugh. 'Wendy,' he laughed. 'I do believe I have shut her up in the drawer!'

Peter let poor Tink out of the drawer and she flew about the nursery screaming with fury. Peter said he was sorry. 'How could I know you were in the drawer?' he said.

'Peter,' said Wendy, 'if only she would stand still and let me see her.'

Now fairies hardly ever stand still, but for a moment Tinker Bell came to rest on the cuckoo clock. 'Tink,' said Peter to the fairy. 'This lady says she wishes you were her fairy.'

Tinker Bell snapped an answer in fairy talk. She was still very angry and Wendy asked what she had said.

'She is not being very polite,' he said. 'She says you are a great ugly girl and that she is my fairy. But she knows she cannot be my fairy because I am a gentleman and she is a lady.'

Tink turned in disgust. 'You silly ass,' she said to Peter and disappeared into the bathroom. Tink always called people 'You silly ass'. It was her favourite expression.

'She is quite a common fairy really,' said Peter. 'She's called Tinker Bell because she mends the pots and kettles, like gypsy tinkers do.'

Wendy and Peter Pan were now sitting in the armchair and she was still full of questions. 'If you don't live in Kensington Gardens now . . .'

Peter Pan interrupted her. 'Sometimes I still do . . .'

'But where do you live mostly now?'

'With the lost boys,' answered Peter.

'Whoever are they?' said Wendy.

'They are the children who fall out of their prams when their nurses are looking the other way. If they are not claimed in seven days, they are sent far away to the Neverland. I'm their captain'.

Wendy thought what fun it must be, but she could not see how cunning Peter Pan was. He said Neverland was rather lonely because there were no girls. 'They are far too clever to fall out of their prams,' he said. 'So they never get lost and never come to Neverland.'

Wendy was so pleased to hear Peter Pan's words. 'I think,' she said, 'it is perfectly lovely the way you talk about girls. My brother John over there hates girls.'

Peter leapt from the chair and kicked John out of bed, blankets and all. John was so deeply asleep he didn't even wake

up, but continued dozing on the floor. Wendy told Peter off for
kicking her brother. 'You are not the captain in this house,'
she said.

But Wendy realized that Peter only meant to be kind to her
and told him he could kiss her. 'I thought you would want it
back,' he said a little bitterly, offering to return the thimble.

'Oh dear,' said Wendy, still not wanting to hurt Peter's
feelings. 'I don't mean a kiss, I mean a thimble.'

She kissed Peter on the cheek to show him how. Immediately
he said he would also give her a thimble. But before he could
kiss her, Wendy let out a screech. Someone was pulling her hair.

It was Tink. She was angrier than ever and Peter had never
seen her so naughty before. Before flying off in a flash of light,
the fairy spoke to him sharply.

'Tink says she will do that every time you give me a thimble,'
explained Peter.

Wendy asked why and Peter questioned Tink. 'You silly ass,'
was all Tink would say. Peter did not understand, but Wendy
somehow knew what was wrong. Tinker Bell was jealous of her
giving thimbles to Peter.

Peter soon forgot about Tinker's fury and began telling
Wendy why he came to the nursery window. It was not to see
her, but to listen to the stories Mrs Darling read to the children.
'You see,' said Peter, 'I don't know any stories. Nor do any of
the lost boys.'

'How awful,' said Wendy.

'Do you know,' Peter asked, 'why swallows build nests in the
eaves of houses? It is to listen to the stories children are told at
night. That reminds me, your mother was telling a lovely story
the other night.'

Wendy asked which one it was and Peter said it was about
a prince who couldn't find the lady who wore the glass slipper.
'Oh, that was Cinderella,' said Wendy. 'The prince found her,
and they lived happily ever after.'

Peter seemed delighted to hear the story had a happy ending
and he rushed towards the window. 'Where are you going?'
asked Wendy.

'To tell the other boys what happened to the prince.'

'Don't go, Peter,' she begged. 'I know lots of stories.'

That was exactly what Wendy said, so there can be no doubt
about it. Wendy first put the idea into Peter's head. 'Come with
me then, Wendy,' he said. 'Come with me to Neverland and tell
your stories to the lost boys.'

He began to pull her towards the window.

'No. No. I can't. Think of mummy! Besides I can't fly.'

'I'll teach you,' said Peter. 'I'll show you how to jump on the wind's back and then away we go.'

'Oo! How lovely to fly,' said Wendy.

'Wendy, Wendy,' said Peter. 'When you are sleeping in your silly bed, you could be flying about with me saying funny things to the stars.'

'How lovely,' said Wendy.

'And, Wendy, there are mermaids.'

'Mermaids! What, mermaids with tails?'

'Such long tails,' said Peter.

'Oh,' cried Wendy, 'to see a mermaid.'

Peter Pan was being so cunning. He was saying everything to tempt Wendy into coming away with him. 'You could tuck us in at night. You could darn our clothes and make pockets for us. None of us has any pockets.'

Everything he said excited her so much. 'Oo! To fly! To see mermaids with tails!' she cried. 'Peter, would you teach John and Michael to fly too?'

'If you like,' said Peter, without much interest, and Wendy ran and shook her brothers awake.

'Wake up,' she cried. 'Peter Pan has come to teach us to fly.'

John rubbed his eyes. 'Then I shall get up,' he said. Of course, he was already on the floor. 'Hallo,' he said. 'I am up!'

Michael was up, too. But then Peter Pan suddenly signalled to everyone to be quiet. They listened but could hear nothing. Everything must be right. No, stop! Everything was wrong. Nana, who had been barking all evening, was quiet now. It was her silence they had heard.

'Quick! Hide!' cried John. They were just in time.

Nana burst into the nursery dragging the servant Liza behind her. Liza glanced around and the nursery looked its old self. You would have sworn its three wicked inmates were sleeping angelically, when they were really artfully hidden behind the window curtains.

Liza was in a bad mood. She had been making Christmas puddings in the kitchen and had been forced to leave her work because Nana had been barking so much. 'There, you suspicious brute,' she said, looking around the darkened room and hanging on to the rope holding Nana. 'The children are perfectly safe. The little angels are sound asleep in bed.'

Nana tried to free herself from Liza's clutches because she

knew all was not right. She could hear the children breathing behind the curtains. But Liza hauled the dog away. Unhappy Nana was tied up again. 'Any more barking,' said Liza, 'and I'll go and get the master to whip you.'

Nana cared little whether she was whipped or not, as long as her children were safe. She barked and barked, and strained and strained at the chain . . .

*   *   *

John was the first to emerge from behind the curtains. 'Peter,' he said. 'Can you really fly?'

Peter did not answer but took off and flew once around the room. 'How wonderful,' said John.

It looked so easy that the children all tried it. But they always went down instead of up. 'How do you do it?' asked John.

'You just think wonderful thoughts,' explained Peter, 'and they lift you into the air.'

Of course, Peter was trifling with the children, for no one can fly unless fairy dust has been blown on them. Fortunately Peter's hands were still covered in fairy dust from carrying Tinker Bell and he blew some on the children. 'Now just wriggle your shoulders and let go,' said Peter.

They were all on their beds and gallant Michael let go first and immediately he soared towards the nursery ceiling.

'I flew!' he screamed, while still in mid-air.

John and Wendy also let go and soon they were soaring towards the bathroom.

'Oh, lovely,' said Wendy.

'Oh, ripping,' said John.

'Look at me,' cried Michael.

'Look at me!' they all shouted.

They could not fly so well as Peter, their heads kept bobbing against the ceiling. Peter tried to help Wendy but he had to stop because Tinker Bell grew so angry.

'I say,' cried John. 'Why don't we all go out?'

Of course this was what Peter Pan had been planning, but Wendy still hesitated. Peter knew what to do. 'Mermaids!' he said again.

'Oo,' said Wendy, so excited.

Michael was ready. He wanted to see how long it took to fly

a billion miles.

'And there are pirates,' added Peter for good measure.

'Pirates!' shouted John, seizing his Sunday hat. 'Let us go at once.'

* * *

Meanwhile Nana had been desperately pulling at the rope tied to the chain in the yard. At last it broke. In a moment she had run to No. 27, burst through the front door and galloped into the dining room. Her paws were raised to the heavens.

Mr and Mrs Darling knew at once that something terrible was happening in the nursery and, without another thought, rushed into the street.

They looked up to the nursery window and saw that it was still safely shut. But the room was ablaze with light, and the most heart-gripping sight of all, they could see in shadow on the curtain three figures in night attire circling round and round, not on the floor but in the air.

But wait! Not three figures, four!

The Darlings opened their front door but even as they were coming up the stairs, the stars once more blew the nursery window open and the smallest star of all called out: 'Watch out, Peter!'

Peter knew there was not a moment to lose. 'Come,' he cried and soared out into the midnight sky, followed by John, Michael and Wendy.

Mr and Mrs Darling and Nana rushed into the nursery too late. The birds had flown.

CHAPTER FOUR

The Flight to Neverland

'Second to the right, and straight on till morning.' That, Peter had told Wendy, was the way to Neverland. But even birds, carrying maps and looking at them at windy corners, could not have found their way with those directions. Peter, you must understand, often said anything that came into his head.

At first Wendy, John and Michael trusted Peter completely, and so great were the delights of flying that they wasted time circling round church spires and any other tall objects which took their fancy.

Wendy was the first to worry about how long they had been gone from No. 14. John began to think, too. They were flying over a sea and he could not decide whether it was their second sea or their third night. Sometimes it was dark, sometimes light. Sometimes they were cold because they were in their nightclothes. Sometimes they were hot. Did they feel hungry at times, or were they merely pretending because Peter had such a wonderful way of feeding them?

He chased birds which had food in their mouths and snatched it from them. Then the birds would follow and try and snatch it back. They happily chased each other for miles.

Certainly they did not pretend to be sleepy. They were sleepy, and that was dangerous. The moment their eyes closed, down

they fell. The awful thing was that Peter thought it so funny.

'There he goes again,' he would cry out in delight, as Michael suddenly dropped like a stone.

'Save him. Save him,' shouted Wendy. Eventually Peter would dive through the air and catch Michael just before he hit the sea. He always waited until the very last moment, and you felt it was his cleverness which interested him and not the saving of a human life.

Peter could sleep in the air without falling by simply lying on his back and floating, but then he was so light that if you got behind him and blew he went faster.

Peter loved playing games. Sometimes he would fly close to the water and touch each shark's passing tail, just like children running their fingers along iron railings in the street.

'Tell him to stop showing off,' said John.

Wendy said they should be nice to Peter in case he left them, but Michael thought they could always go back.

'How could we ever find our way back without him?' said Wendy.

'Well, then, we could go on,' said John.

'That is the awful thing,' said Wendy. 'We would have to go on because we don't know how to stop.'

The truth was that Peter had forgotten to tell them how to stop.

John said that if the worst came to the worst, all they had to do was to go straight on. The world was round, he said, and in time they must get back to their nursery window.

Wendy asked how they were going to feed themselves but John said that he had already nipped a bit of food from an eagle's mouth. 'After the twentieth try,' said Wendy, 'and besides see how we keep bumping into clouds.'

Indeed they were always bumping into things. They could now fly straight, although they still kicked too much. But if they saw a cloud in front of them, the more they tried to avoid it, the more certain they were to bump into it.

If Nana had been there she would have had a bandage around Michael's head by now.

*   *   *

Sometimes Peter forgot all sorts of things. He would go so fast
that he would suddenly shoot out of sight, to have some
adventure by himself. He would return, laughing over something
fearfully funny he had been saying to a star, but had already
forgotten what it was. Or he would come back with mermaid
scales still sticking to him, and yet not be able to say for certain
what had happened.

'If he forgets things so quickly,' warned Wendy, 'we can't be
sure that he won't forget us.'

Indeed sometimes when he returned he did not remember
them, at least not well. Once even Wendy had to tell him her
name. He just told her to keep reminding him if he did forget in
future.

But Peter did not forget to teach them to sleep in the air,
showing them how to lie out flat on a strong wind that was going
their way. The children found they could sleep quite safely.
They would have slept more but Peter quickly tired of sleeping
and he would cry out in his captain's voice: 'We get off here.'
Then the children would wake and change winds to head off
towards their destination.

So with occasional arguments, but on the whole plenty of
laughing and rollicking, they came close to the island of
Neverland. It was many moons before they reached it and their
finding it was not so much due to Peter or Tink's guidance, but
because the island was out looking for them. No one can find
the magic shores unless the island finds them.

'There it is,' said Peter calmly.

'Where, where?' the children cried.

'Where all the arrows are pointing,' said Peter.

A million arrows of light from the sun were pointing out the
island to the children. The sun wanted them to be sure of their
way before leaving them for the night.

All three children stood on tiptoe in the air to get their first
sight of the island. Strange to say they recognised it at once.
It looked like a friend they knew so well.

'John,' cried Wendy, 'there's the lagoon!'

'I say, John, I see your flamingo,' said Michael.

John could see Michael's cave and Michael spotted Wendy's
orphan wolf. Michael also saw the redskin camp and John asked
him where because he wanted to see if the braves were on the
warpath. 'I see now,' he said. 'Yes, they are on the warpath
right enough.'

Peter was a little annoyed that they seemed to know so much

about the island. He wanted everything to be his big surprise. But soon they needed his help again. Night fell, leaving the island in gloom. In the old days at home the Neverland had always begun to look a little threatening by bedtime and the children were always glad when mother put the night-lights on. As darkness fell they had liked Nana saying that Neverland was all make-believe.

Of course Neverland had been make-believe in those days, but it was real now. There were no night-lights, and it was getting darker every moment. And where was Nana?

They flew close to Peter and saw that his careless manner had gone. They were now over the fearsome island, flying so low that sometimes a tree top grazed their faces. They could not see anything horrid in the air, yet flying grew harder, as though they were pushing their way through enemy forces. Sometimes they hung in the air until Peter had beaten back the air with his fists. 'They don't want us to land,' he explained.

'Who are they?' Wendy whispered with a shudder.

But Peter could not or would not say whether it was the fairies fighting them. Instead he asked John: 'Do you want an adventure now, or would you like to have tea first?'

Wendy and Michael wanted 'tea first', but John asked what sort of adventure.

'There's a pirate asleep in the grass below,' said Peter. 'If you like we could go down and kill him.'

'What! Do you kill many?' asked John.

'Tons,' said Peter. 'I have never known so many pirates on the island before.'

'Who is their captain now?' asked John.

'Hook,' said Peter, his face becoming very serious as he said the hated name.

'James Hook?' asked John, nervously.

'Aye,' said Peter.

Michael began to cry, and even John could only speak in gulps, for they both knew of Hook's infamy. 'He was Blackbeard's bo'sun,' John whispered. 'He is the most terrible of all the pirates.'

'How big is he?' asked John.

Peter surprised him by saying that Hook was not as big as he had been. 'I cut a bit off him,' said Peter.

'What bit?' asked John.

'His right hand.'

'Then he can't fight now?' said John, much relieved.

'Oh, can't he just,' said Peter. 'He has an iron hook instead of a right hand, and he claws with it.'

'Claws!' shuddered John.

'Yes. And there is one thing you must promise me. If we meet Hook in open fight, you must leave him to me.'

'I promise,' said John, loyally.

At that moment they were not too worried about Hook and the other dangers which lurked below because Tink was flying with them. They could see each other in her light. She could not fly as slowly as the children and had to go round and round them in circles. So the children were travelling down a brightly lit tunnel. Wendy quite liked this until Peter pointed out a problem.

'Tink tells me that the pirates sighted us before darkness came and they got Long Tom out.'

'The big gun?' asked John.

'Yes,' said Peter, 'and of course they must see Tink's light. They are sure to fire at us.'

'Tell Tink to go away,' said the three children together.

Peter refused. 'She is also rather frightened. You don't think I would send her away all by herself in such a state.'

Just then someone gave Peter a loving pinch.

'Then tell her to put out her light,' suggested Wendy.

Peter said that she could not do that. 'That is about the only thing fairies can't do. It just goes out by itself when she falls asleep, same as the stars.'

'Then tell her to go to sleep at once,' John ordered.

'She can't sleep except when she's sleepy. It is the only other thing fairies can't do.'

'Seems to me,' yawned John, 'sleeping is the only thing worth doing.'

This time it was John's turn to get a mysterious pinch, but it was not a loving one.

'If only one of us had a pocket to put her in,' said Peter.

They all searched but they could not find a pocket between them. Then Peter solved the problem. Tink could travel in John's hat. Tink agreed and they flew on in the dark with Wendy carrying the mischievous fairy in the hat. Tink hated being carried by Wendy.

As they flew on everything fell silent. It was the quietest silence they had ever heard, broken only by a distant lapping sound. Peter explained it was wild beasts drinking. A little later they heard a sound like branches of a tree rubbing together.

'It's the redskins sharpening their knives,' said Peter.

Everything was too quiet for Michael. 'If only someone would make a real noise,' he said.

'BOOM!' The air was shattered by a tremendous crash. The pirates had fired on them with Long Tom. The blast from the explosion sent everyone flying across the heavens. No one was hit but Peter was carried far out to sea, John and Michael found themselves alone in the darkness, while Wendy was blown upwards with no companion but Tinker Bell. It would have been wiser if Wendy had dropped the hat then and there.

I don't know whether the idea came suddenly to Tink, or whether she had planned it on the way, but she popped out of the hat and began to lure Wendy to her destruction.

Tinker was not all bad. It's just that she was all bad just then. Sometimes she was all good. Fairies have to be one thing or the other, because being so small they only have room for one feeling at a time. Just then she was full of jealousy over Wendy.

Tink flew back and forth, signalling to Wendy to follow her. What else could Wendy do? She called out to Peter and John and Michael, but only received echoes in return. She did not know that Tink hated her at that moment, and followed the fairy to her doom.

CHAPTER FIVE

The Island of Neverland

Whenever Peter Pan returns to Neverland, the island wakes up again. When he is not there, the fairies take an hour longer to get up in the morning, the redskins never stop eating, and when the pirates and the lost boys meet they never bother to fight each other. When Peter returns the whole island comes to life.

On the night of Peter's return everyone was on the move. Put your ear to the ground and you can hear the whole island buzzing with activity.

The lost boys were out looking for Peter, the pirates were out looking for the lost boys, the redskins were looking for the pirates, and the beasts were looking out for the redskins. They were all going round and round the island, but they did not meet because they were travelling at the same speed and in the same direction.

All wanted blood except the lost boys. They liked blood normally, but tonight they are out to greet their captain, Peter Pan. As all the different groups follow each other tonight, let us take a look at them one by one.

The number of boys on the island varies. It depends on who's been killed and who's growing up, which is against Peter's rules. He thins them out from time to time. Tonight there are six boys. Let us watch them as they pass by in single file, each with a dagger in his hand.

They all wear the skins of bears which they have killed themselves. Peter makes sure they all wear the skins, because no one is allowed to look like him.

First of all there is Tootles, the gentlest and saddest of the boys. He is also rather brave but has had fewer adventures than the other boys. It is just that when things happen, he always seems to have just stepped round the corner to do something. When he comes back from collecting sticks, or whatever, the other boys would be sweeping up the blood. But he had better watch out tonight because Tinker Bell is bent on mischief and she needs help. Tink thinks he's the most easily tricked of the boys.

Next comes Nibs, a cheerful lad, and then there is Slightly, who always thinks he can remember when he was a baby in the days before he was lost. He cuts whistles out of tree branches and dances to his own tunes. He is the most conceited of the boys.

Now here is Curly. He is forever in trouble, often taking the blame for other boys' naughtiness. If Peter ever asks, 'Who did this?' then Curly is the one who will step forward.

Finally there are the Twins. We cannot describe what they are like for fear of describing the wrong one. They are so alike. Peter never quite understood what twins were and because his band were never allowed to know anything he did not know, no one knew much about the twins.

As the boys vanish into the gloom, not far behind them come the pirates, always singing the same dreadful song:

'Avast below, yo ho, heave to,
A-pirating we go,
And if we're parted by a shot,
We're sure to meet below!'

There never was a more villainous-looking lot, armed to the teeth with pistols, cutlasses and daggers. There was the handsome Italian Cecco, with great arms bare and pieces of eight in his ears as ornaments. He had once cut his name in letters of blood on the back of the prison governor at Goa.

Behind Cecco is the gigantic Blackamoor, followed by Bill Jukes, who has tattoes all over him. Cookson, said to be the evil Black Murphy's brother, is next.

Then comes Gentleman Starkey, once a high-born schoolboy but now a man with many a dainty way of killing his enemies.

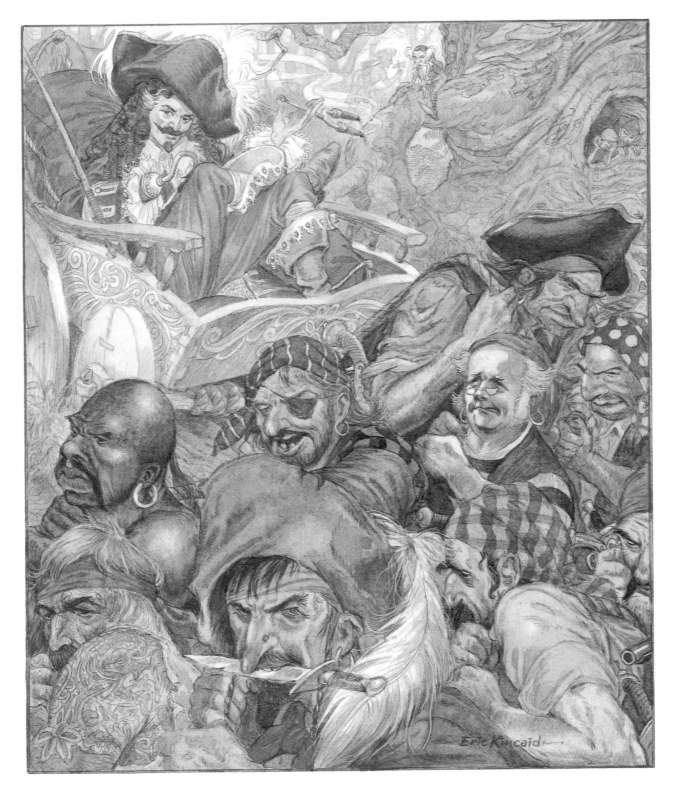

There never was a more villainous-looking lot,
armed to the teeth with pistols, cutlasses and daggers.

Behind him comes Skylights and the Irish bo'sun Smee, a strangely friendly man who often apologised to any man he was about to kill.

Noodler, a man who always looked as though his hands were fixed on backwards, comes next, closely followed by Robert Mullins, Alf Mason and other ruffians well-known and dreaded on the Spanish Main.

In the middle of this gang of villians, resting in a rough chariot pulled by his men, is the blackest and most terrifying of all the pirates, James Hook. Instead of a right hand, he has an iron hook which he raises into the air to get his men to travel more quickly. He treats them like dogs and as dogs they obey him utterly.

Hook is a huge man with a dark evil face and hair dressed in long curls, just like old King Charles II. His blue eyes can look quite sad, but when he plunges his hook into anyone, two red spots appear in them. His eyes light up terribly. The most awful thing about Hook, apart from his grim hook, is that the more villainous he becomes, the more politely he behaves.

Tonight he lies in his chariot smoking two cigars at once in a gadget he invented himself.

Yet, he is a breed apart from his men. It is rumoured he went to the most famous school in England before he became a pirate. He is a man of great courage and they say the only thing which frightens him is the sight of his own blood, which is thick and strangely coloured. But there is one other thing which terrifies Captain James Hook. We will learn about that later.

But before the pirates disappear into the dark in search of the boys, let us kill a pirate to show how Hook works. Skylights will do. As they travel on, Skylights accidentally lurches against Hook and ruffles his lace collar. Hook is furious. His hook shoots out, there is a tearing sound and a single screech. Then the body is kicked aside and the pirates move on. Hook has not even taken the cigars out of his mouth.

Such is the terrible man against whom Peter Pan must pit his wits.

On the trail of the pirates, stealing silently down the war-path, come the redskins. They carry tomahawks and knives, and their naked bodies gleam with paint and oil. They are the Piccaninny Tribe and, strung around their bodies, are the scalps of boys as well as pirates. Leading is the brave Great Big Little Panther, who has so many scalps that they are weighing him down. At the end of the column comes Tiger Lily, the most beautiful redskin princess.

The redskins pass by in a ghostly silence. They are so clever they can step on a broken twig without making a sound. The only noise is their heavy breathing because they are still so fat from eating too much while Peter was away.

Coming out of the shadows after the redskins are the beasts, a procession of lions, tigers, bears and other savage animals. Their tongues are hanging out tonight because they are hungry.

When they have passed, there is still one more creature to come, a gigantic crocodile.

* * *

So the island and its inhabitants are on the move. All are keeping a sharp look out at the front, but no one suspects that the danger may be creeping up from behind.

The first group to fall out of the moving circle were the boys. They sat down on the grass close to their underground home, and began to talk about when they thought Peter would return.

'I do wish he would come back soon,' said the boys, who although they obeyed their captain without question, were all larger than him.

'I am the only one who is not frightened of the pirates,' said Slightly, 'but I wish he would come back and tell us whether he has heard anything more of Cinderella.'

Tootles was sure that Cinderella must be very much like his mother. It was only when Peter was away that they could talk about their mothers. Peter said mothers were silly and should not be spoken of.

The boys' talk suddenly came to a halt when they heard a chilling distant sound. It was a grim song they knew too well:

> 'Yo ho, yo ho, the pirate life,
> The flag of skull and bones,
> A merry hour, a hempen rope,
> And hey for Davy Jones.'

Now, where are the lost boys? Rabbits could not have disappeared more quickly. All the boys, except Nibs who had gone off to look for the pirates, had disappeared into their underground home. But how did they get in? Look closely and you may see seven trees, each with a hollow trunk as large as a boy. These are the seven entrances to the home which Hook has been searching for many a moon.

As the pirates advanced, the quick eye of Starkey saw Nibs disappearing through the wood. He had his pistol out in a flash. But quicker still was Hook's iron claw, which snapped around Starkey's shoulder.

'It was one of the boys you hate,' said Starkey. 'I could have shot him dead.'

'Put that pistol back,' snarled Hook threateningly. 'The sound of your shot would have brought Tiger Lily's redskins on us. Do you want to lose your scalp?'

Smee jumped forward. 'Shall I after him, captain?' he said. 'I'll tickle him with my Johnny Corkscrew.' Smee had names for everything and his gleaming cutlass was called Johnny Corkscrew because he wiggled it in the wound. One could mention some lovely habits of Smee. For instance after killing someone he would wipe his spectacles instead of his cutlass.

'Not now,' said Hook darkly. 'That was only one of the boys. I want to capture all seven. Now! Scatter and look for them.'

The pirates disappeared into the trees and Hook was left alone with Smee. 'There are seven of them,' said the black captain. 'But the one I really want is Peter Pan. 'Twas he who cut off my arm. I've waited long to shake his hand with this. Oh, how I will tear him apart.'

Hook devilishly brandished the hook.

'I have often heard you say how useful the hook is,' said Smee. 'Didn't you say once that if you were a mother you would want all your children born with a hook instead of a hand.'

Hook looked proudly at his hook and then his black look returned. 'Peter flung my arm,' he said wincing, 'to a passing crocodile.'

'I have often noticed,' said Smee, 'your strange dread of crocodiles.'

'Not of crocodiles,' said Hook. 'But of that one crocodile. It liked my arm so much, Smee, that it has followed me ever since, from sea to sea, and from land to land, licking its lips for the rest of me.'

'In a way,' said Smee, 'that is a sort of compliment.'

'I want no compliments,' barked Hook. 'I want Peter Pan, who first gave the brute its taste for me. But then I do have an advantage over it. It once swallowed a clock which goes tick inside it. So before it can reach me I hear the tick and run off.'

Hook laughed deep and long and sat down on a large mushroom. 'Some day that clock will run down,' said Smee, 'and then the crocodile will get you.'

Hook wetted his dry lips. 'Aye. That's the fear that haunts me.'

Suddenly Hook stood up. 'Odds, bobs, hammer and tongs!' he shouted. 'I'm burning!'

He examined the mushroom he was sitting on and found it was hot. Hook kicked it and it fell over. Beneath it was a hole and smoke was billowing out of it.

The pirates looked at each other and both exclaimed: 'It's a chimney!' Not only was smoke coming out, but also the sound of children's voices. They knew at once they had discovered the lost boys' home. They bent down and listened to the boys chatting cheerfully below.

They listened for a few moments before replacing the chimney, noticing at the same time the seven entrances to the hollow trees. Each one looked far too small for either Hook or Smee to get down. 'Did you hear them say Peter Pan was still away?' asked Smee.

Hook nodded and stood for a long time, lost in thought. Then at last a blood curdling smile lit up his swarthy face. 'We will return to the ship and cook up a large rich cake with green sugar on it,' he sneered. 'We will leave it on the shores of the mermaids' lagoon for the boys to find.'

Hook knew the boys had no mothers so they would not know how dangerous it was to eat such a special cake. 'They will gobble it up,' he laughed, 'and they will all die. Ho, ho, ho.'

The two pirates celebrated the idea by breaking into song again:

> 'Avast below, when I appear,
> By fear they're overtook,
> Nothing's left upon the bones when you,
> Have shaken claws with Hook.'

But another tune stopped them in their tracks. 'Tick! Tick! Tick! Tick!' Hook stood shuddering and shaking in fear, one foot in the air.

'The crocodile,' he gasped and bounded away.

The crocodile had passed the redskins and was now on the trail of Hook.

Soon after, the boys emerged into the open to find Nibs rushing back towards them, pursued by a pack of wolves. 'Save me. Save me,' he cried, falling on the ground.

'What would Peter do?' said one boy.

'He would turn his back on them and look through his legs,' said another.

One by one they bent over and looked through their legs at the approaching wolves. Victory came quickly. The wolves took one look at the boys, dropped their tails and fled.

Now Nibs rose from the ground and, looking to the sky, shouted: 'I have seen a wonderful thing. A great white bird is flying this way.'

'What is it?' cried the other boys.

'I don't know,' said Nibs, 'but it looks so weary and it keeps saying "Poor Wendy".'

'I remember,' said Slightly, pretending he could still remember his babyhood, 'there are birds called Wendies.'

'Here it comes,' said Curly.

Wendy was now overhead and the boys could hear her cries. But louder still came the shrill voice of Tinker Bell. The jealous fairy was pinching Wendy at every chance.

'Hallo, Tink,' welcomed the boys.

Tink's reply rang out for all to hear. 'Peter wants you to shoot the Wendy.'

No boy would ever disobey Peter. All but Tootles, who already had his bow and arrow in hand, popped down their trees to find weapons.

'Quick, Tootles,' screamed Tinker Bell. 'Shoot the Wendy bird. Peter will be so pleased.'

Tootles fitted an arrow into his bow, took aim and fired. It flew true and straight. Wendy fluttered to the ground with an arrow in her breast.

CHAPTER SIX

The Wendy House

Foolish Tootles was standing like a conqueror over Wendy's body when the other boys sprang, armed, from their trees.

'You are too late,' he said proudly. 'I have shot Wendy. Peter will be so pleased with me.'

Overhead Tinker Bell shouted 'Silly ass!' and flew off. The others did not hear her as they crowded round Wendy. A terrible silence fell upon the wood and if Wendy's heart had been beating, they would have all heard it.

'This is no bird,' said Slightly. 'I think it must be a lady.'

'And we have killed her,' said Nibs.

Every boy took off his hat as a mark of respect there and then. 'Now I see,' said Curly, sadly. 'Peter was bringing her for us.'

'A lady to look after us at last,' said one of the twins, 'and Tootles has killed her.'

They were sorry for Tootles, but sorrier for themselves. Tootles' face was very white. 'I did it,' he said. 'When I dreamed of ladies I used to think my mother had come. But when at last she did come, I shot her.'

He moved sadly away, but, feeling sorry for Tootles, they called him back. 'No, I must go,' he said. 'I am so afraid of Peter.'

It was at this tragic moment that they heard a sound which brought their hearts to their mouths. It was Peter crowing.

'Hide her!' whispered the boys, gathering around Wendy. But Tootles stood aside.

Then Peter was down beside them. 'Greetings, boys,' he said, and they all saluted him in silence. Peter frowned. 'I am back. Why don't you cheer? I have some great news. I have at last brought a mother for you all. Have you seen her?'

Tootles spoke so quietly. 'I will show her to you. Stand back boys. Let Peter see.'

Peter looked at the figure of Wendy, knelt down and removed the arrow from her breast. 'Whose arrow?' he asked.

'Mine, Peter,' said Tootles, who sunk to his knees.

Peter raised the arrow in the air ready to strike the poor boy. Tootles, who thought he should die for what he had done, bared his chest and told Peter to strike him dead. But as hard as he tried, Peter could not bring the arrow down. Something stopped him.

'Look!' said Nibs. 'It's the Wendy lady. Look at her arm.'

They looked and saw that Wendy had raised her arm. As Nibs bent down, two whispered words came to her lips: 'Poor Tootles.'

'She lives,' said Peter, kneeling down beside her. That's when he saw the acorn button which he had given Wendy in the nursery. She had hung it on the chain around her neck. 'See!' he cried. 'The arrow struck against the button. It is the kiss I gave her. It has saved her life.'

'I remember kisses,' said Slightly. 'Let me see that button. Yes, that is definitely a kiss.'

Peter begged Wendy to get better. 'Remember,' he said. 'I must show you the mermaids.'

Just then there was a cry in the sky. 'It's Tink,' said Curly. 'She is crying because Wendy lives.'

The boys then had to tell Peter of Tink's crime and he looked up into the sky in fury. 'Listen, Tinker Bell,' he said. 'I am your friend no longer. Be gone for ever.'

Tinker Bell flew down onto his shoulder and begged to be forgiven. Peter brushed her off. But when Wendy moved her arm again he forgave Tink a little. 'Well, not forever, but for a whole week.'

Tink left and the boys said they should move Wendy to their home to recover. But Peter said it was not right to carry a lady anywhere. 'We will build a house round her,' he announced.

In a moment they were scurrying round making Wendy more comfortable, preparing a bed and building a fire. As they worked John and Michael appeared. They were so tired they dragged their feet behind them, falling asleep at one step and then waking at the next.

'Hello, Peter,' they said.

'Hello?' said Peter, who had quite forgotten them.

'Is Wendy asleep?' they asked.

Peter said she was and continued measuring Wendy to see how big the house would have to be. 'Curly,' he said. 'Make sure that these two boys help with the new house.'

'Build a house?' asked John.

'For the Wendy,' said Curly.

'For Wendy,' John said in disbelief. 'Why, she is only a girl.'

'That,' explained Curly, 'is why we are her servants.'

'You? Wendy's servants!' said John and Michael together.

'Yes,' said Peter, 'and you will be, too. To work with you. We'll make a table and some chairs first and then build the house round them.'

'Yes,' said Slightly, 'that is how a house is built. It all comes back to me now.'

The astonished brothers were dragged away to cut wood and carry while Peter ordered Slightly to go and find a doctor. Slightly disappeared, wondering where he would find a doctor. He scratched his head and came up with an idea. He returned a few moments later wearing John's hat and looking very serious, just like a doctor would do.

'Please, sir,' said Peter, approaching Slightly, 'are you the doctor?'

The difference between Peter and the other boys was that they knew when something was make-believe or not, while to Peter make-believe and true were exactly the same. This worried the boys because sometimes they had to eat make-believe suppers, and Peter would always rap their knuckles if they did not pretend to make-believe properly.

'Yes, I am the doctor,' said Slightly. 'I will put a glass thing in the patient's mouth.'

Peter waited anxiously as Slightly put a glass thing in Wendy's mouth and then removed it. 'How is she?' asked Peter.

'I think it has cured her,' said the doctor.

'Good,' said Peter.

'I will call again this evening,' said Slightly, 'but in the meantime you must give her beef tea from a cup with

a spout on it.'

Then, with a very polite good-bye to Peter, the doctor left. Slightly heaved a sigh of relief that Peter had really believed he was the doctor.

By the time the doctor had finished his business, all the materials for Wendy's house were ready. 'But what sort of house would Wendy like?' wondered Peter. Just then Wendy moved and began to sing very quietly:

> 'I wish I had a pretty house,
> The littlest ever seen,
> With funny little red walls,
> And roof of mossy green.'

Everyone was delighted and that is how they built Wendy's house. They were so happy, they sang as they worked.

> 'We've built the little walls and roof,
> and made a lovely door
> So tell us, mother Wendy,
> What are you wanting more?'

Wendy answered them with another verse:

> 'Oh, really, next I think I'll have,
> Gay windows all about,
> With roses peeping in, you know,
> And babies peeping out.'

There were not any roses, babies neither. So they completed the house with make-believe and sang a little more:

> 'We've made the roses peeping out,
> The babies are at the door,
> We cannot make ourselves, you know,
> 'Cos we've been made before.'

When all was done, Peter, seeing that the house was such a good idea, immediately pretended that it was his own, marching up and down ordering all sorts of finishing touches. Tootles gave up the sole of his shoe for a knocker and John's hat, with the top knocked through, made for a very good chimney. And as if to agree, the hat immediately began to smoke.

Now all that was left to do was to knock on the door and ask who was inside. 'You must always look your best when you knock at someone's door,' said Peter, smartening himself up.

Then, as Tinker Bell sneered from a nearby branch, Peter knocked on the door and all the boys wondered who would come out. The door did open and a lady did come out. It was Wendy and they all lifted their hats to her.

'Where am I?' she asked.

'You are in the house we built for you,' said Slightly.

'It's a lovely, darling house,' said Wendy.

'And we are your children,' cried the twins.

Then they all went on their knees and begged Wendy to be their mother. 'I'm only a little girl,' said Wendy, 'but I do feel that a mother is exactly what I am.'

'You are! You are!' they all cried.

'Very well,' she said. 'I will do my best. Come inside, you naughty children, and before I put you to bed, I just have time to finish the story of Cinderella.'

In they all went. I don't know how there was room for them, but you can squeeze very tight in Neverland. That was the first of many happy evenings they had with Wendy.

Later that night she tucked them up in the great bed in their home under the ground, but she herself slept in the little house. Outside Peter kept watch with his sword drawn because he could hear the pirates singing far away and he knew the wolves were on the prowl.

The little house looked so cosy and safe in the darkness with a bright light showing through the blinds, the chimney smoking beautifully and Peter standing guard outside.

Of course, Peter did not stay on guard very long. He was soon asleep and the fairies of the night took great delight in tweaking his nose as they passed by on their way home to their nests in the tops of the trees.

CHAPTER SEVEN

The Home under the Ground

The first thing Peter did the next day was to measure Wendy, John and Michael for hollow trees. Peter thought it safer for John and Michael to live with the boys in the home under the ground, although Wendy slept in her own house at night. Each tree had to fit exactly the person who was to use it and each person had to have his own tree. No two people were quite the same size.

Once you fitted a tree you drew in breath at the top and down you went at exactly the right speed, while to come up, you breathed in and out alternately and wriggled up. Once you mastered the art it was easy.

Peter measures people as carefully as for a suit of clothes. The only difference is that clothes are made to fit you, while you have to be made to fit the tree. If you are bumpy in awkward places or the only available tree is an odd shape, then Peter does some things to you, and after that you fit. Wendy and Michael fitted their trees at the first try, but John had to be altered a little.

After a few days' practice they could all go up and down as gaily as buckets in a well. And how they came to love their new home, especially Wendy.

It consisted of only one room and on the floor grew stout mushrooms which were used as stools. A Never tree tried to grow in the centre of the room, but every morning the boys sawed the trunk through, level with the floor. By tea-time it had always grown two feet high again and then they put a door on top of it, so making a table. As soon as things were cleared away, they sawed off the trunk again to make more room to play.

There was an enormous fire-place which could be lit in almost any part of the room you chose. Wendy dried the boys' clothes over it. The bed leaned against the wall by day and was let down in the evening. It filled nearly half the room. All the boys except Michael slept in it, lying like sardines in a tin. There was a strict rule against turning around in the night. The person who wanted to roll over had to give a signal, and then they would all turn over at the same time.

Michael should have used the bed, but Wendy would insist on having a baby, and as he was the littlest he was hung up in a basket.

There was one small opening in the wall, no larger than a bird-cage. This was the private apartment of Tinker Bell. It could be shut off from the rest of the home by a tiny curtain, which Tink, who was most fussy, always kept drawn when dressing or undressing. No woman, however important or rich, could have had a more beautiful bedroom. There were different bedspreads to match the fruit-blossom of the season, wonderful carpets and rugs and even a twinkling chandelier, although of course she lit the room herself.

Tink was very vain about her appearance and spent a lot of time looking in her fine mirror. All in all the room was so smart, it gave the appearance of having a permanently turned-up and very snooty nose.

Wendy was kept so busy by the boys, cooking, sewing, darning and telling stories. Really, there were whole weeks when she never went above ground during the day. The cooking in particular kept her nose to the pot. Their main food was roasted bread-fruit, yams, coconut, baked pig, mammee apples, tappa rolls and bananas washed down with calabashes of poe-poe. But you never knew whether there would be a real meal or just make-believe. It all depended on Peter's whim. He could eat, really eat, but make-believe was so real to him that he got fatter even if the meal was not a true one.

Now, do you remember Wendy's pet wolf? Well, it soon

discovered that Wendy had come to the island and found her. They fell into each other's arms like old friends. Afterwards it followed her everywhere.

As the time passed, Wendy did think about her mother and father at No. 14. She did not really worry because she was absolutely sure they would always keep the nursery window open for her return. What did disturb her at times was that John remembered his parents only vaguely, like people he had once known. Michael, still so young, was quite happy to believe that Wendy was his real mother.

These things frightened her and she tried to get them to remember their old lives by setting examination papers on it. The questions were quite ordinary – 'What was the colour of your Mother's eyes? Who was taller, Father or Mother? Was Mother blonde or brunette? Write an essay of How I Spent My Last Holiday. Describe Mother's laugh. Describe Mother's party dress. Describe the Nursery Kennel and its occupant.'

When they could not answer a particular question Wendy put black marks on the paper. What a dreadful number of black marks John had. But worse still, Slightly wanted to reply to every question too and he was sure he would come first in the exam. Sad Slightly came out last.

*   *   *

Adventures for the lost boys and the children were a daily event, but Peter also invented a new game which fascinated him a great deal. He pretended to have the sort of adventures which Wendy, John and Michael had at their real home.

He would sit on a stool throwing a ball to the others, playfully run around the house pushing everyone about or even go out for walks, pretending they were good for his health. He would return without having so much as killed a grizzly bear. But Peter could not do such boring things for long.

He often went out alone and when he came back no one was sure whether he had had an adventure or not. Sometimes he might have forgotten what he had done, and when you went out you found the body. On the other hand he might tell about a great adventure and you never did find the body.

Sometimes he came in with his head bandaged and Wendy would bathe the wound in lukewarm water. She was never quite

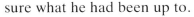

sure what he had been up to.

But there were adventures which had to be true because the children were involved in them. To describe them all would take a huge book, so the most we can do is to give an example of an average hour on the island. Should we tell the story of the brush with the redskins at Slightly Gulch? That was the day Peter decided to change sides in the middle of the fight.

With victory still in the balance, Peter called out to Tootles: 'I'm a redskin, what are you?' Tootles followed his captain, as did the others. They all became redskins. The fight would have ended there had not the real redskins joined in with Peter's game and agreed to be lost boys for that one time.

But there were other adventures. There was the night attack by redskins on the home under the gound. That was when several redskins got stuck in the hollow trees and had to be pulled out like corks.

Then there was that poisonous cake the pirates cooked to give to the lost boys. They placed it in one cunning spot after another, but Wendy always found it first and snatched it from the hands of her children. Eventually the cake became rock hard and Captain Hook used to trip over it in the dark.

Tinker Bell was involved in one particular adventure. While Wendy was asleep she and some other fairies lifted her onto a large leaf and let her float away from the island towards the mainland. Luckily the leaf sank and Wendy woke and swam back to safety.

There was the day Peter challenged lions to attack him. He drew a circle around him on the ground with an arrow and defied the beasts to cross it. Though he waited for hours, with the boys looking on breathlessly from nearby trees, not one lion dared cross the line.

On another occasion, a Never bird built a nest in a tree overhanging the lagoon. Then the nest with its eggs fell into the water, but it kept floating. The mother bird would not leave her eggs and she continued to sit on the nest, floating wherever the tide took her. Peter, who it must be said used to take great pleasure in tormenting the bird, ordered that she should not be disturbed in future. The Never bird would reward Peter for his kindness one day.

But the most exciting adventure concerned Peter Pan and Tiger Lily, the beautiful redskin princess. It all took place at Mermaids' Lagoon.

The children often spent long summer days on the lagoon, swimming and trying to play with the mermaids. You must not think the mermaids were friendly, on the contrary. Wendy never had a pleasant word with any of them. She would creep up to Marooners' Rock where the mermaids loved to sun themselves, combing out their hair in a lazy way which quite irritated her. But as soon as Wendy got close, they dived into the water, splashing her with their tails, not by accident, but on purpose.

The mermaids treated all the boys in the same way, except, of course, Peter. He chatted with them at Marooners' Rock and even sat on their tails when they were cheeky. He did give Wendy one of their combs.

The most haunting time at which to see the mermaids is in the evening when the moon slowly rises into the sky and the mermaids howl with the strangest cries. The lagoon is a dangerous place for mortal beings then. Wendy had never been by the lagoon at that time because she had a strict rule that all the boys should be in bed by seven o'clock.

But one day Wendy and the boys were all on Marooners' Rock. She was doing some sewing while most of the boys were snoozing in the sunshine.

As she stitched, a change came over the lagoon. Little shivers ran over it, the sun vanished and dark shadows stole across the lagoon. It turned cold and so dark that Wendy could not see what she was doing any longer. When she looked up the lagoon was not the friendly place she had known.

It was not, she knew, that night had come, but that something as dark as night had come. She should have woken the children immediately, but she did not. Even when she heard the sound of muffled oars, and her heart was in her mouth, she did not wake them.

Wendy was frozen to the spot, remembering only how Marooners' Rock had got its name. On that rock, evil captains had left sailors to drown. For when the tide rises, the rock is soon under water.

It was lucky for the boys that there was one among them who could sniff danger even in his sleep. Peter Pan sprang up wide awake and stood absolutely still with one hand to his ear, listening.

'Pirates!' he cried.

*The most haunting time at which to see the mermaids
is in the evening . . .*

CHAPTER EIGHT

The Mermaids' Lagoon

Peter Pan's cry of 'Pirates!' woke all the other boys and they gathered round him. A strange smile came to Peter's face and when Wendy saw it she shuddered. She knew he was looking forward to another great adventure. While that smile remained on his face, no one dared say a word. All they could do was to stand ready to obey. The order came sharply: 'Dive!'

Everyone dived in the water, leaving the lagoon seemingly deserted. Marooners' Rock stood alone in the forbidding waters, almost as if it was marooned itself.

The boat drew nearer. It was the pirate dinghy with three figures aboard – Smee, Starkey and none other than Tiger Lily. Her hands and ankles were tied and she knew her fate. She was to be left on the rock to drown, a death more terrible than by fire or torture because her tribe believed that there is no path through water to the happy hunting-ground. Yet her face did not show any fear. She was the daughter of a chief and she would die honourably as a chief's daughter.

The pirates had caught Tiger Lily creeping around their ship with a knife in her mouth. No watch was kept on the ship because it was Captain Hook's boast that just the sound of his name was enough to keep people away. So she had easily slipped aboard.

In the gloom the two pirates did not see the rock until they crashed into it. 'Luff, you lubber,' cried Smee. 'Here's the rock. Now, then, what we have to do is to put the redskin on it, and leave her to drown.'

The princess was brutally thrown onto the rock.

Quite near the rock, but out of sight, two heads bobbed up and down in the water, Peter's and Wendy's. Wendy was crying because it was the first tragedy she had seen. Peter had seen many tragedies, but he had forgotten them all. He was just angry that it was two against one; two pirates against the beautiful Tiger Lily, the redskin Princess he now meant to save.

Peter could have waited until the pirates had gone, but he was never one to choose the easy way. As usual he had a plan. He would imitate the voice of Hook.

'Ahoy there, you lubbers,' he called. It was a marvellous imitation.

'The captain!' said the pirates, staring at each other in surprise.

'He must be swimming out to us,' said Starkey, when they had looked for him in vain. Then Smee called out to tell his captain that they had put Tiger Lily on the rock.

'Set her free,' came the astonishing answer.

'Free?' The pirates scratched their heads in amazement.

'Yes, cut her bonds and let her go.'

'But, captain . . .'

'At once, do you hear,' shouted Peter, 'or I'll plunge my hook into you.'

'This is strange,' gasped Smee.

'Better do what the captain orders,' said Starkey, a little nervously.

'Aye, aye,' said Smee, and he cut Tiger Lily's ropes. She immediately slipped into the water.

Wendy thought Peter had been so clever, but she also knew he would be so cock-a-hoop at his own success in fooling the pirates that he would crow out in delight. So she covered his mouth with her hand.

Peter may have been about to crow but his lips puckered into a whistle of surprise when suddenly he heard Hook's voice. 'Boat ahoy!' came the shout over the water. It was not Peter speaking. The real Captain Hook was also out and about on the lagoon.

Hook was swimming to the boat and his men raised a lantern to show him the way. In the light Wendy saw his hook grip the

boat's side. For the first time she saw the evil swarthy face as Hook rose dripping from the water. Quaking in fright, she would have liked to swim quickly away. But Peter would not move. He was just too full of himself. 'Am I not a wonder? Am I not a real wonder?' he whispered. 'Now let's listen to what Hook has got to say.'

The two pirates were very curious to know why their captain had come, but he just sat with his head on his hook looking deeply miserable.

'Captain, is all well?' they asked. Hook did not answer, but his moans and sighs could be heard clearly.

'He sighs,' said Smee.

'He sighs again,' said Starkey.

'And yet a third time he sighs,' said Smee. 'What's up, captain?'

'The game's up,' he cried. 'Those boys have found a mother.'

Frightened though she was, Wendy was proud to hear Hook's words.

'A mother?' cried Starkey. 'This is indeed a bad day.'

'What's a mother?' asked the ignorant Smee.

Wendy could not believe Smee did not know what a mother was. She always said afterwards that if you could have a pet pirate, Smee would be her one.

Just then Peter pulled Wendy beneath the water because he thought Hook had spotted them. 'What was that?' cried Hook, hearing the water ripple.

'I heard nothing,' said Starkey, raising the lantern over the waters. As the pirates looked they saw a strange sight. It was the floating nest of the Never bird and she was sitting on it.

'See,' said Hook, his voice breaking softly as if he was remembering his more innocent days as a boy. 'That is a mother. The nest must have fallen into the water, but would she desert her eggs? Never!'

Smee gazed at the bird in amazement, but Starkey was more suspicious. 'If that bird is a mother, perhaps she is hanging around here to help Peter.'

Hook winced. 'Yes, that is the fear which haunts me.'

Just then Smee suggested something which cheered Hook greatly. 'Captain,' he said, 'why don't we kidnap the boys' mother and make her our mother?'

'It's a princely scheme,' cried Hook. 'We will seize the children and carry them to the boat. We will make the boys walk the plank and she can be our mother.'

It was too much for little Wendy. 'Never!' she blurted out.

'What was that?' cried the three pirates together.

They looked but could still see nothing. It must have been the wind, they decided as the boat gently bumped into Marooners' Rock. Hook suddenly remembered Tiger Lily. 'Where is the redskin?'

Hook had a mischievous sense of humour sometimes and the two men thought he was joking with them. 'It's all right, Captain, we let her go,' said Smee.

'Let her go!' roared Hook.

''Twas your own orders, captain,' said Smee, beginning to worry.

'You called over the water to us. You told us to let her go,' said Starkey.

'Brimstone and gall,' thundered Hook. 'What mischief is afoot here.' His face had gone black with rage, but he could see that his two men were not lying. 'Lads,' he said. 'I gave no such order.'

'Then something very odd's been going on here,' said Smee.

Hook's voice quivered a little as he turned towards the lagoon. Beads of cold sweat glistened on his brow. 'Spirit that haunts this dark lagoon tonight,' he cried. 'Do you hear me?'

Of course Peter should have kept quiet, but he didn't. He immediately answered in Hook's voice. 'Odds, Bobs, hammer and tongs, I hear you.'

Hook did not blink, but Smee and Starkey clung to each other in terror. 'Who are you stranger? Speak,' Hook demanded.

'I am James Hook,' replied the voice, 'Captain of the Jolly Roger.'

'You are not. You are not!' Hook cried hoarsely.

'Brimstone and gall,' the voice answered. 'Say that again and I'll spike you with an anchor.'

Hook changed his tack. 'If you are Hook, who am I?'

'A codfish,' came the reply. 'Only a codfish.'

'A codfish!' Hook echoed. He saw the two men draw back, looking at him most strangely. They were wondering whether their captain really was a codfish.

Hook began to think he was losing his mind. But he was not beaten yet. He began a guessing game. 'Hook,' he called out. 'Have you another voice?'

Peter could never resist a game and he answered quite naturally in his own voice. 'I have.'

'And another name?'

'Spirit that haunts this dark lagoon tonight,' he cried.
'Do you hear me?'

'Aye, aye.'

'Vegetable?' asked the real Hook.

'No.'

'Mineral?'

'No.'

'Animal?'

'Yes.'

'Man?' asked Hook.

'No!' said Peter indignantly.

'Boy?'

'Yes.'

'Ordinary boy?'

'No!'

'Wonderful boy?' asked Hook.

Wendy winced as Peter answered: 'Yes.'

Hook was still puzzled. 'You ask him some questions,' he said to the others, wiping the chilling sweat from his brow. The pirates could not think of anything to ask.

'Can't guess?' crowed Peter. 'Can't guess? Do you give up?'

Peter had given the pirates their chance. 'Yes, yes, we give up.'

'Well, then,' he cried proudly. 'I am Peter Pan.'

Pan! Peter Pan! In a moment Hook was himself again. 'Now we have him,' he shouted. 'Take him, dead or alive.'

Hook dived into the lagoon at the very moment Peter cried out: 'Are you ready boys?'

'Aye, aye,' came the reply from all around the lagoon.

'Then let's have at them,' cried Peter, seeing the boys burst from all corners of the lagoon.

The fight was short and sharp. First to draw blood was John, who bravely climbed into the boat and attacked Starkey. There was a fierce struggle as John tore his cutlass from him. Starkey wriggled overboard and John leapt after him as the dinghy drifted away.

Tootles led the attack on Smee and was slightly wounded in the ribs by the pirate's corkscrewing cutlass. But Smee himself was bloodied by Curley. Further from the rock, Starkey had escaped from John and was now battling Slightly and the twins. When Starkey swam off again, the boys found themselves surrounding Hook.

They were all brave boys and should not be blamed for backing away from the pirate captain as his swirling iron claw made a circle of dead water round him. The boys fled like fishes.

But there was one who did not fear him; there was one prepared to enter the circle. But strangely Peter and Hook did not meet in the water. Hook clambered onto the rock to catch his breath and at that moment Peter climbed on at the other end. The rock was slippery and they had to crawl rather than climb. Neither knew that the other one was coming.

Each feeling his way in the darkness, it was not until they actually grabbed each other's arm by accident and came face to face, that they met.

Peter was not scared. He gnashed his teeth with joy at meeting his enemy. Thinking very quickly, he snatched a knife from Hook's belt and was about to drive it home, when he saw that he was higher up the rock than his foe. It would not have been fair, so he gave the pirate a hand to help him up.

It was then that Hook bit him. It was not the pain but the unfairness of it which dazed Peter, especially after he had helped Hook up the rock. The shock of Hook's unfair play made him quite helpless. Twice the iron hand clawed him. Peter seemed doomed to die by the dreaded hook.

'Tick! Tick! Tick! Tick!' Hook heard the familiar sound with dread. A few moments later the boys saw Hook in the water striking out wildly for the ship. There was no look of triumph on his face, just pure fear. The crocodile was on his tail!

Normally the boys would have swum alongside cheering, but now they were searching for Peter and Wendy, calling out over the lagoon.

There was no answer, just the mocking laughter of the mermaids. 'They must be swimming back, or flying,' the boys decided. They were not worried because they had such faith in Peter. They just chuckled, knowing they would be late for bed; and it was all Mother Wendy's fault.

* * *

When the voices of the boys had died away, a cold silence came over the lagoon, and then a feeble cry was heard. 'Help! Help!'

Two small figures were in the water beside the rock. Wendy had fainted and lay in Peter's arms. With one last effort Peter pulled her up on the rock and then lay down beside her. He saw that the water level was rising fast and knew they would soon be drowned. Peter Pan would be no more.

As they lay side by side, a mischievous mermaid caught

Wendy by the feet, and began pulling her softly into the water.
Peter, feeling her slip from him, was just in time to drag her
back. But he had to tell her the truth.

'We are on the rock, Wendy,' he said. 'But it is growing
smaller. Soon the water will cover it. We must go.'

'Yes,' said Wendy quietly. 'Shall we swim or fly, Peter?'

'Could you swim or fly as far as the island without me?'
he asked.

She had to admit that she was too exhausted and Peter's head
sunk at the answer. 'I can't help you,' he said. 'Hook wounded
me. I can neither swim or fly.'

'Do you mean we will both be drowned?'

They put their hands over their eyes to avoid looking at the
rising water. As they waited for the end, something brushed
against Peter. It was as light as a kiss and it stayed on his cheek,
as if to say: 'Can I help?' It was the tail of a kite which Michael
had made a few days earlier. In a high wind it had torn itself out
of his hand and floated away.

'Michael's kite,' said Peter, looking up at the fluttering object.
'If it lifted Michael off the ground, why should it not carry you?'

'Both of us,' said Wendy.

'It can't lift two,' said Peter. 'Michael and Curly tried.'

'Let us draw lots,' said Wendy bravely.

But Peter was already tying the tail of the kite round her. At
first she refused to go without him, but then with a 'Goodbye'
he pushed her from the rock. In a few minutes she was carried
out of his sight. Peter was alone on the rock.

The rock was a very small one now and soon it would be
under water. Pale rays of light tiptoed across the lagoon and
Peter heard the saddest and most musical sound in the world,
the mermaids calling to the moon.

The sound even frightened Peter a little. But that did not stop
him from standing up and boldly saying: 'To die will be a very
big adventure.'

CHAPTER NINE

The Never Bird

Peter was quite alone on Marooners' Rock and he saw the mermaids, one by one, swimming off to their bedchambers. They spend the night in coral caves, and the door to each one has a tiny bell on it. Every time the doors open or shut the bell rings out. Peter heard the bells ring from the sea bottom as the mermaids went off to bed.

The water around Marooners' Rock rose until it was lapping at Peter's feet. To pass the time until he was finally swallowed up, Peter watched the only thing moving on the lagoon. He thought it was a bit of floating paper, perhaps part of the kite. He wondered idly how long it would take to drift ashore.

But soon after he noticed an odd thing. Whatever was moving out there had a purpose because it was fighting the tide. Peter, always happy to support the underdog, could not help clapping each time the piece of paper gained a few yards against the tide. It was such a brave piece of paper.

It was not really a piece of paper; it was the Never bird, sitting on her nest, making desperate efforts to reach Peter. By flapping her wings, she was somehow able to guide her strange boat. By the time Peter saw her she was absolutely exhausted. She had come to save him, even if it meant losing the eggs she was sitting on. It was the bird's way of thanking Peter for ordering everyone to leave her in peace when the nest fell in the water.

The Never bird called out to Peter, trying to tell him what she was doing. Peter shouted back, asking what she was doing. Now, many people think that birds and strange boys like Peter can understand each other's languages, but the truth must be told. Not only could they not understand each other, they also forgot their manners.

'I . . . want . . . you . . . to . . . get . . . into . . . the . . . nest . . .,' the bird called, speaking as slowly and distinctly as possible. 'I . . . am . . . too . . . tired . . . to . . . bring . . . it . . . any . . . nearer . . . Can . . . you . . . swim . . . to . . . me?'

'What are you quacking about?' said Peter.

The Never bird became irritated. They do have very short tempers. 'You dunderhead little boy,' she screamed. 'Why don't you do as I tell you?'

Peter was sure she was calling him names and shouted at her again. Then they both snapped at each other.

'Shut up!'

'Shut up!'

Nevertheless the Never bird was determined to save Peter and with one last mighty effort, she paddled herself to the rock. Then up she flew, deserting her eggs.

At last Peter understood and clutched the nest and jumped aboard, waving his thanks to the bird which now fluttered overhead. Like a worrying mother, she wanted to see what he did with her eggs.

There were two large white eggs and Peter lifted them up. The bird covered her face with her wings. She could hardly bear to see what happened to her eggs, but she could not help peeping through her feathers.

Peter was busy thinking. He had seen the old pole which had been driven into Marooners' Rock long ago to mark the site of buried treasure. The children had discovered the glittering hoard and, when in playful mood, used to fling showers of diamonds, pearls and pieces of eight at the gulls. Thinking it was food, the gulls would pounce on the gems and then fly away in a rage at the scurvy trick which had been played on them.

But the pole was still there and on it Starkey had hung his wide-brimmed tarpaulin waterproof hat. Peter put the eggs in the hat and pushed it out onto the lagoon. It floated beautifully.

The Never bird saw at once what he was up to and flew down and once more settled snugly on her eggs. Meanwhile Peter got into the nest, took the pole as a mast and hung up his shirt for a sail.

*Meanwhile Peter got into the nest, took the pole
as a mast and hung up his shirt for a sail.*

The Never bird drifted in one direction and he floated off in another, both cheering each other for being so clever, though Peter thought he had been especially smart.

When Peter reached dry land, he left the nest where the Never bird would quickly find it. But the hat was such a fine nest that she abandoned the nest altogether.

In days to come when Starkey walked by the shores, he would look out jealously at the bird sitting in his hat. And, strange to tell, all Never birds now build their nest in the shape of a broad-brimmed hat.

*   *   *

There was great rejoicing when Peter reached the home under the ground. Wendy had got back already and every boy had adventures to tell. Perhaps the best thing was that all of them were several hours late for bed. In fact they tried everything to stay up even later, demanding bandages for make-believe wounds.

Wendy, who was so happy to have everyone at home again, would have none of it. 'To bed! To bed!' she ordered in a voice that had to be obeyed.

Next day, however, she let them have their way. She gave out bandages to everyone, and they played until bedtime at a special game of limping about and carrying their arms in slings.

CHAPTER TEN

The Happy Home

The most important result of the adventure on Mermaids' Lagoon was that the redskins became the boys' greatest friends and allies. Peter had saved Tiger Lily from a dreadful fate, and now there was nothing she and her braves would not do for him.

All night they sat above the home under the ground, guarding everyone against the big attack by the pirates, which clearly was going to come very soon. In the meantime they smoked their peace pipes.

They called Peter the Great White Father, and almost worshipped him. Peter liked this tremendously. 'The Great White Father,' he would say, 'is glad to see the Piccaninny warriors protecting his wigwam from the pirates.'

'Me Tiger Lily,' the princess would say. 'Peter Pan save me, me his best friend. Me no let pirates hurt him.'

'It is good,' Peter would say. 'Peter Pan has spoken.'

That meant that it was time for the redskins to shut up. And they always obeyed. But they did not treat the other boys with such respect. They looked on the boys as very ordinary braves and said 'How-do?' to them and things like that. The boys did not like it, but Peter thought it quite right that they should be treated in a less important way.

Secretly Wendy sympathized with the boys a little, but she was too loyal a housewife to listen to any complaints against father. 'Father knows best,' she always said. But her private opinion was that the redskins should not call her squaw.

The redskins were at their posts above the home one evening when the children were having their evening meal. Peter had gone out to find the time for Wendy. The way you got time on the island was to find the crocodile and then stay near it until the clock struck the hour.

The meal happened to be a make-believe tea, and they all sat round the table guzzling everything they could imagine. They were in a boisterous mood, chattering and playing about. The noise was deafening. If Wendy had said 'Silence!' once, she had said it twenty times.

Sometimes there were disputes between the boys. But it was a golden rule that no one could hit back during meals. Instead they had to shout, 'I complain of so-and-so', and Wendy would settle the argument.

'Have you finished your milk, yet?' she asked Slightly.

'Almost,' said Slightly, looking into his imaginary mug.

'No, he hasn't,' said Nibs. 'He hasn't even begun to drink it.'

That was enough to cause a fight and Slightly seized his chance. His hand shot into the air. 'I complain of Nibs,' he cried.

John's hand, however, was up first. 'May I sit in father's chair?'

Wendy was shocked. 'Certainly not. Only father can sit there.'

'He is not really our father,' said John. 'He didn't even know what a father was until I told him.'

The twins decided John was grumbling far too much. 'We complain of John,' they cried.

Tootles held up his hand. 'I don't suppose I could be father,' he said very quietly.

Wendy was always very gentle with Tootles. 'No, I'm afraid you can't.'

Tootles said very little, but once he had said something he had a silly way of going on. 'Then, if I can't be father, I don't suppose, Michael, you would let me be baby?'

'No, I won't,' said Michael, who was already in his hanging basket.

'If I can't be a baby,' said Tootles, 'can I be a twin?'

'No,' replied the twins. 'It's awfully difficult to be a twin.'

Tootles did not give up. 'If I can't be anything important,

would any of you like to see me do a trick?'

'No!' they all replied.

Then they all set about each other, shouting, arguing, squabbling and, of course, complaining.

'I complain of the twins.'

'I complain of Nibs.'

'I complain of Curly.'

So much noise, so much fun. 'Oh. Oh dear,' said Wendy at last. 'I'm sure I sometimes think that children are more trouble than they are worth.'

Wendy told the boys to clear away and sat down at her work basket. There was a huge collection of socks to darn and every pair had holes in the toes.

Then it was Michael's turn to grumble. 'Wendy,' he said. 'I'm too big for this cradle.'

'You must stay there,' said Wendy. 'You are the smallest boy here and there must always be a baby in a cradle in every house.'

That put Michael in his place and the other boys began to dance. It was such a happy scene which met Peter on his return. He brought nuts for the boys and the right time for Wendy. 'You really spoil the boys,' she said.

'Aye, old lady,' said Peter.

'It was me who told Peter mothers are called old lady,' said Michael.

'I complain of Michael,' said Curly instantly, thinking he was boasting. But there was no time to listen to his complaint because the first twin went up to Peter and said everyone wanted to do some more dancing.

'Dance away, my little man,' said Peter, who was in great spirits.

'But we want you to dance,' said the twin.

Peter was really the best dancer of all but he was in playful mood. 'What, me!' he cried. 'My old bones would rattle.'

'But it's Saturday night,' said Slightly. 'You must dance.'

It was not really Saturday night. At least it might have been, but they had long lost count of the days. But if anyone wanted to do something special they always said it was Saturday night.

'Of course it is Saturday night, Peter,' said Wendy.

So they all danced that night and later, as the boys got ready for bed, Peter and Wendy talked. 'I was just thinking,' he said. 'It is only make-believe that I am their father?'

'Oh, yes,' said Wendy.

'You see,' he went on, 'it would make me seem so old if I was their father.'

'But the boys do belong to us,' said Wendy. 'They are yours and mine.'

'But not really,' said Peter, a little worried.

'Not if you don't want them to be,' answered Wendy, hearing Peter sigh with relief. 'But what do you really think of me?'

'I am your devoted son,' said Peter.

Wendy had guessed as much. Peter would always be a boy, even if she would have liked him to grow up. Peter's mother she would have to be.

'It's very odd,' said Peter. 'You are the same as Tiger Lily. She doesn't want to be my mother either. Perhaps Tinker Bell will be my mother.'

Tink had only one answer. 'You silly ass.'

Wendy had heard Tink say the words so often that she now knew what they meant. 'I almost agree with her,' said Wendy.

When the children were ready for bed, they had more dances. Wendy sang a song and it was such a haunting tune that the children danced, pretending to be afraid of their own shadows. Little did they know that other more frightening shadows would soon be on them.

But for that moment all was to be fun. They danced, sang, fought with pillows and tried to tell stories.

Even Slightly tried to tell a story that night, but the beginning was so terribly dull that even he found it boring. 'Yes, it is a dull story,' he confessed. 'Let's pretend my beginning is the end.'

And then at last they all got into bed to listen to Wendy's story. It was the story the boys loved best, and the one Peter hated most. Usually when she began this story he left the room or put his hands over his ears. If he had done either, things might have turned out differently. But tonight, the Night of Nights as they came to call it, he remained on his mushroom stool to listen.

CHAPTER ELEVEN

Wendy's Story

'Listen then,' said Wendy, settling down to tell her story with Michael at her feet and the other boys in bed. There was once a gentleman . . .'

'I wish it was a lady,' interrupted Curley.

'I wish he'd been a white rat,' said Nibs.

'Quiet!' said Wendy. 'There was a lady, too.'

'I hope she isn't dead,' said Tootles.

'Oh, no, she's not dead,' said Wendy.

'A little less noise from you, children,' called out Peter, who was determined that Wendy should finish the story, however boring he thought it was.

'The gentleman's name,' continued Wendy, 'was Mr Darling, and her name was Mrs Darling.'

'I think I knew them once,' said Michael, a little unsure.

'They were married, you know,' said Wendy, 'and what do you think they had?'

'White rats,' cried Nibs, inspired.

'No,' said Wendy. 'They had three children and those three children had a faithful nurse, a dog called Nana. But Mr Darling was angry with Nana one day and chained her up in the yard, and so all the children flew away. They flew away to the Neverland where the lost children are.'

'I thought that's what they did,' said Curly, excitedly. 'I don't know how, but I just knew they did.'

'Oh, Wendy,' cried Tootles. 'Was one of the lost children called Tootles?'

'Yes, of course he was.'

Tootles was overcome with excitement. 'I'm in a story, Nibs. I'm in a story!'

'Hush,' said Wendy. 'Now I want you to think how unhappy Mr and Mrs Darling were after their children flew away. Think of the empty beds.'

'It's terribly sad,' said one of the twins.

'I don't see how this story can have a happy ending,' said the second twin. 'Do you Nibs?'

Wendy went on. 'If you know how great a mother's love can be, you should not be frightened how this story will end.'

Peter hated talk of mothers, and he really disliked this part of the story. 'You see,' said Wendy, 'the heroine of this story knew that her mother would always leave the nursery window open so the children could fly back in. That's why these children stayed away for years and had a lovely time.'

'Did they ever go back?' asked Slightly.

Wendy was not ready to give the ending of the story away so quickly. 'Let's take a peep into the future,' she said. 'The years have rolled by and who is this elegant lady I see. I don't know how old she is but I see her getting off a train at London station . . . '

'Oh, Wendy, who is she?' cried Nibs excitedly, as if he didn't know.

'Can it be,' said Wendy, screwing up her eyes to look closer. 'Can it be . . . yes . . . no . . . yes . . . it is Wendy.'

Cries of delight echoed from the big bed.

'And who are the two noble gentlemen I see with her?' continued Wendy. 'Can they be John and Michael? They are!'

'Oh,' cried the boys.

'You see, dear brothers,' she said looking at John and then Michael. 'The window was still open. The children were right to trust in their mother's love. The children flew back to their mother and father and I cannot describe how happy the scene was.'

That was Wendy's story and everyone except Peter enjoyed it. He let out a sad groan.

'What is it, Peter?' asked Wendy.

'It's a pain,' he said.

'What kind of pain is it?' said Wendy.

Peter Pan said it was not so much a pain as an ache in his heart. 'Wendy,' said Peter. 'You are wrong about mothers.'

What Peter said frightened the children and they all gathered around him to hear something he had never told them before. 'Long ago,' he said, 'I thought like Wendy. I thought my mother would always keep the window open for me. So I stayed away for moons and moons before flying back. But I found the window was barred. My mother had forgotten all about me and there was another little boy sleeping in my bed.'

Now, whether this was true is another matter. But at that moment Peter thought he was telling the truth. 'Are you sure mothers are like that?' asked the boys.

'Yes, indeed,' answered Peter.

'Mothers are toads then,' said the boys.

John and Michael cried out as one. 'Wendy, let us go home.'

'Yes,' she said, clutching both of them in her arms.

'No, not tonight,' said the lost boys.

'Yes, we must go at once,' said Wendy. 'Perhaps mother already thinks we are never coming back.'

The sudden sadness at that thought made Wendy forget Peter's feelings, and she said to him quite sharply: 'Peter, will you make the necessary arrangements?'

'If you wish it,' he replied, as coolly as if she'd asked him to pass the nuts. He was not going to show he cared if Wendy didn't.

There was not so much as a "sorry-you're-going" from either of them. But of course he cared very much. Peter was feeling very angry about grown-ups who, as usual, seemed to be spoiling everything. 'I'll go and make the arrangements,' said Peter, hurrying to his tree. Once inside he took a series of quick breaths. In the Neverland there is a saying that every time you breathe a grown-up dies. Peter was killing them off as fast as he could.

When Peter left, the lost boys began to panic about losing Wendy. 'We can't let her go,' said one.

'Let's keep her prisoner,' said another.

'Aye. Chain her up.'

Wendy turned to Tootles for help. He might have been the silliest boy but he knew what to say. 'I am just Tootles, and nobody ever listens to me. But the first boy who does not behave like a gentleman towards Wendy will have a bloodied nose from me.'

The others stood back uneasily and just then Peter returned.
They knew they would get no support from him. He would
never keep a girl in the Neverland against her will.

'Wendy,' he said, striding up and down unhappily, 'I have
asked the redskins to guide you through the wood, as flying tires
you so much.'

Wendy thanked him and Peter gave Nibs orders to wake
Tinker Bell. Nibs had to knock twice before he got an answer,
though Tink had really been sitting up in bed listening for some
time.

'You are to get up, Tink,' said Nibs. 'Peter wants you to take
Wendy on a journey.'

Tink had been delighted to hear that Wendy was going, but
she was jolly sure that she wasn't going to be the one to take
her. So she snapped angrily at Nibs and pretended to go to sleep
again.

Peter heard what had been going on and marched to the
young fairy's bedroom. 'Tink,' he said, 'if you don't get up and
dress at once, I will open the curtains and then we will all see
you in your night-dress.'

That made Tink leap to the floor. 'Who said I wasn't getting
up?' she cried.

Meanwhile the boys were looking sadly at Wendy, John and
Michael, now ready for the journey. They were sad and
dejected, not just because they were about to lose their mother,
but also because they thought she was going off somewhere nice,
somewhere they had not been invited.

Wendy felt a tear coming into her eye. 'Dear ones,' she said.
'If you all come with me, I'm sure my father and mother would
adopt you. You could all stay at my house.'

The invitation was meant especially for Peter, but each of the
boys was thinking just of himself. They jumped at the invitation.
'Peter, can we all go?' they asked.

'All right,' said Peter, bitterly. 'You can go.' The boys rushed
away to get their things packed, leaving Wendy and Peter
together.

Wendy was determined to give Peter some medicine before
they all set off. She loved to give the boys medicine and really
gave them far too much. It was only water but she poured it
from the kernel of a fruit and counted out the drops. This made
it always seem like real medicine.

Wendy was ready to give it to Peter when she saw such a sad
look on his face. 'Come on Peter,' she said. 'Pack your things

and we'll be away.'

'No,' he replied. 'I'm not going with you, Wendy. Who knows, if I did, I might be forced to grow up. I want to stay a boy and have fun.' Then he skipped up and down the room, pretending to play merrily on his pipes. She actually had to run after him to say one more thing.

'We could find your mother,' she said softly.

Now, Peter, if ever he really did have a mother, no longer missed her. He could do very well without one, and he said so. Wendy tried to persuade him once more but it was no good. Peter's mind was made up. 'Peter isn't coming,' she explained to the lost boys.

Each now carried their things, wrapped in a bundle tied to the end of a stick. 'If you find your mothers,' said Peter, 'I hope you'll like them. Now then, no fuss or crying, good-bye.'

Wendy had to shake his hand as there was no sign he would prefer a thimble. 'You will remember to keep your clothes clean, Peter,' she said. 'And make sure you take your medicine.'

An awkward pause followed and Peter broke the silence by calling for Tink. 'Are you ready, Tinker Bell?'

'Aye, aye,' replied Tink.

'Then lead the way.'

Tink darted up the nearest tree, but no one had the chance to follow because it was at that moment that the pirates made their attack on the redskins. The air was filled with shrieks and the clash of steel.

Below there was dead silence as everyone listened open-mouthed to the battle above. Then Wendy fell on her knees and turned to Peter. Everyone else turned to Peter as if asking him not to desert them now.

As for Peter, he seized his sword. The excitement of battle was in his eye.

CHAPTER TWELVE

The Children are Captured

The pirate attack had been a complete surprise, sure proof that Captain Hook had not played fair. No white man would normally be able to surprise the redskins. The rules of war say that the redskins always attack first, and always at dawn. White man on the other hand is supposed to wait behind his stockade, the young and inexperienced soldiers clutching their revolvers all night, the old hands sleeping, waiting for the coming battle.

As the night passes the redskin scouts wriggle, snake-like, through the grass without stirring one blade. No sound is heard except when they imitate the cry of the coyote wild dogs. Other redskin braves answer as the chill hour before dawn arrives.

That is what is supposed to happen, and the treacherous Hook knew it all too well. So he cannot be excused for breaking all the rules and attacking the redskins as he did that evening; even if some people might say that Hook's diabolical cunning was needed to beat such a clever foe as the redskins.

Many of the redskins went to the happy hunting grounds in the ferocious and sudden attack, but they took some of the pirates with them. Alf Mason died alongside Lean Wolf in battle. George Scourie and Foggerty died too, and Charles Turley fell to the tomahawk of the terrible Panther. It was the Panther who eventually cut an escape path through the pirates for Tiger Lily and the other survivors of the tribe.

Hook, however, was not triumphant in victory. The night's work was not over yet. It was Pan he wanted, Pan and Wendy and their band, but mainly Pan.

Peter was such a small boy and you wonder why Hook hated him so much. True, he had flung Hook's hand to the crocodile. But the truth was that there was something about Peter which sent the pirate captain into a frenzy. It was not Peter's courage, nor his good looks. Actually we all know quite well what it was. It was Peter's cockiness. This had got on Hook's nerves and it made his iron claw twitch. Hook felt like a caged lion being annoyed by a sparrow he could not reach.

The question for Hook now was how to get down one of the trees into the house under the ground, where even now the occupants were wondering who had won the battle. 'We shall soon know,' said Peter. 'The redskins always beat their tom-tom drums if they are victorious in battle.'

Alas, Hook was listening at a tree and heard all. Smee, who was then resting on a tom-tom drum, was ordered to get up and beat it. The sound echoed down into the house. 'The tom-tom!' shouted Peter. 'The redskins have won.'

The doomed children answered with a cheer. It was music to the pirate captain's ears. Hook placed one of his men at each tree and a line of pirates in front, and then, with an evil grimace on his face, he waited.

The children said their farewells to Peter once more and one by one they got into their trees.

* * *

The first to come out was Curly. As he climbed out of his tree, he fell into the arms of the pirate Cecco. He flung him to Smee, who flung him to Starkey, who flung him to Bill Jukes, who flung him to Noodler. He was tossed from one to the other till he fell at the feet of Hook himself. All the boys were plucked from their trees like this, and several of them were in the air at once, like bales of straw being flung onto a stack.

Wendy was treated differently. With that frightening politeness of his, Hook raised his hat to her. Then, offering her his arm, he led Wendy to where the others were being trussed up to make sure none of them could fly away.

All the boys had been tied and gagged, except Slightly. The pirates found that he was like one of those parcels which will

never do up. Which ever way they tried, there never seemed enough rope to go round him. When they tried to pack Slightly in one part, he bulged out in another.

Hook came over to see why Slightly was causing so much trouble. 'Aha,' he cried in triumph, 'I have discovered his secret.'

The truth was that Slightly loved to drink water so much that his stomach had blown up out of all proportion to his proper size. Without telling any of the other boys, he had carved away his tree to make it fit him, rather than reducing himself to fit the tree. Now his tree had been hollowed out enough for even a grown man to slip down. 'That tree will fit me nicely,' sneered Hook.

Slightly was finally tied up and Hook thought for a moment how he would carry all the children away. 'Ho,' he said, looking at the house the boys had built for Wendy. 'That will do.'

The children were thrown into the house and four stout pirates raised it on their shoulders. Then, with the other pirates marching behind and singing their hateful pirate chorus, the procession set off through the wood. Just as the little house disappeared into the forest, the tiny chimney let out a brave little column of smoke as if defying Hook to the last.

Hook saw it as he went about his dastardly business. He tip-toed to Slightly's tree and listened. Not a sound. Was Peter asleep, wondered Hook, or was he waiting at the foot of Slightly's tree with a dagger in his hand? There was no way of knowing except by going down. Hook took off his cloak, slipped into the tree and descended into the unknown.

He arrived at the foot of the tree and in the dim light looked into the room. There on the great bed lay Peter, fast asleep.

Peter had been unaware of the tragedy above. After the children left, he played gaily on his pipes for a while, determined to prove to himself that he did not care a jot about them leaving Neverland. Then he had gone to bed, lying on the top of the cover rather than snugly underneath. He only did that to spite Wendy because she always tucked him up in case the night turned chilly. He saw the medicine that Wendy had left him and he ignored that too.

In truth Peter felt like crying as he began to doze, but he thought it would annoy Wendy more if he laughed instead. So he let out a deep laugh and fell asleep in the middle of it. One arm dropped over the edge of the bed and a leg arched into the air. The unfinished part of his laugh was still on his wide-open

He tip-toed to Slightly's tree and listened.

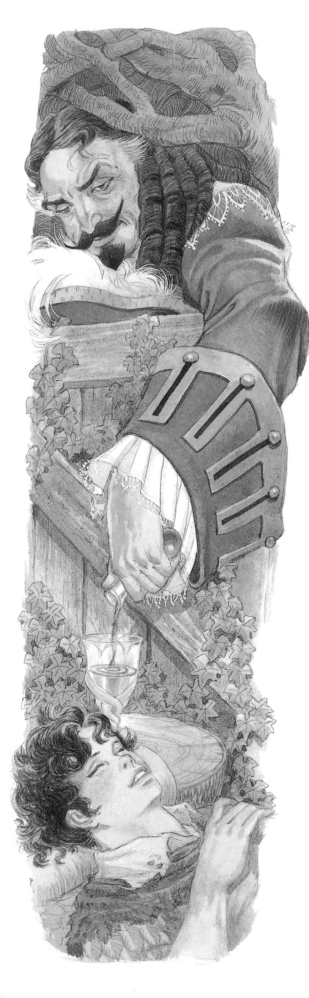

mouth, his pearly teeth gleaming brightly.

Hook looked on and thought for a brief moment what a pretty scene it made. Just sometimes Hook revealed another side to his character. It's said that he liked flowers and gentle music. The man was not all evil. If the nicer side of Hook had been in control then, he might have left Peter to sleep on so peacefully. But he looked again.

Hook saw Peter's smiling open mouth. 'Odds bods,' thought Hook, his black heart taking charge again. 'Pan is so cocky! He's even cocky when he's asleep!'

A light from the lamp shone dimly on the bed, but Hook stood in darkness himself. He stepped forward and found something in his way; the door of Slightly's tree. It did not completely fill the doorway and Hook had been looking over the top of it. Searching for the catch to open it, Hook found to his fury that it was too low down to reach. Angrily he rattled the door and pushed himself against it. It would not budge. Was his enemy to escape him after all?

That was the moment Hook saw Peter's medicine. It was just within reach and an idea came to him. Hook always carried a small bottle containing a deadly poison, just in case he should ever be captured alive. He would rather die by his own hand. Now Hook put five drops of the poison into Peter's medicine glass.

He took one long triumphant look at his victim, as if to say victory was his, and slid up the tree. Donning his hat and wrapping his cloak around him, Hook vanished into the trees muttering to himself in delight at what he had done.

Peter slept on. But just before ten o'clock by crocodile time, he was woken by a gentle tapping on the door of his tree. 'Who's that?' he asked, reaching for his dagger.

There was no answer and he called out once more. Again there was no answer. He got up and went to the door. 'I won't open the door unless you speak,' said Peter.

Then at last he heard a lovely bell-like voice. It was Tink and he quickly undid the door. 'Whatever has happened?' asked Peter.

Tink took a deep breath and, in one long unbroken sentence, told how Wendy and the boys had been captured by the pirates. 'Poor Wendy. I'll rescue her,' cried Peter.

Before setting out he decided to do something to please Wendy. He would take the medicine she had left him. He reached for the glass. 'No!' shrieked Tinker Bell, who had heard

Hook muttering as he sped through the forest. 'Hook has poisoned it.'

'Don't be silly,' said Peter. 'How could Hook have got down here? He's far too big to get down one of our trees. Besides I never fall asleep.'

'I don't know,' said Tink in desperation. 'But he has definitely poisoned your medicine. He has. He has.'

Peter would not listen. He raised the cup and was about to swallow the deadly contents when Tink, in one lightning movement, flew between his lips and drained the glass herself. 'How dare you drink my medicine,' he snapped.

But Tink did not answer. She was already feeling very ill. 'What is the matter with you?' asked Peter.

'It was poisoned,' she said softly, 'and now I am going to be dead.'

'Oh, Tink,' said Peter. 'You drank it to save me. Why?'

Her wings would scarcely carry Tink now, but in reply the adoring fairy dropped onto his shoulder and gave his chin a very loving bite. She whispered in his ear, 'You silly ass' and then fluttered weakly to her room and lay down on the bed.

Peter's head almost filled Tink's room as he looked in and saw that her light was fading. If it went out he knew she would be no more. Peter began to cry huge tears and Tink thought they were so beautiful that she put out her fingers and let the tears flow over them. Then she tried to speak.

Her voice was so low that Peter could hardly hear her. 'Peter,' she said, 'I think I would get well again if the children of the world believed in fairies.'

Peter flung out his arms and called out to all the children: 'Do you believe in fairies?'

Tink sat up in bed to hear her fate. She fancied she heard the children say 'Yes!' But Peter was not sure. He called out again. 'If you believe in fairies, clap your hands. Don't let Tink die.'

This time the sound of distant clapping filled the skies above the house. A few little brats did hiss, but most of the world's children seemed to be clapping that night.

The sound stopped as quickly as it had started, as if every mother had rushed into their children's nursery to discover what on earth was going on. But Tink had already been saved.

Tink's light grew brighter, she sprang from her bed and flashed through the room as cheekily as ever. She did not give a thought to thanking the clapping children who had saved her. And who knows what she would have done if she had got her

hands on the children who hissed.

'Now!' said Peter. 'To rescue Wendy.'

Peter scuttled up his tree. Outside again, he saw that the moon was riding high and snow had fallen on the ground.

He could not be sure where the children had been taken because the snow had hidden all the footprints, and the island was now filled with a deathly silence. He would have liked to wait until morning and daylight, but time was running out.

Just then the crocodile passed him, but not another living thing moved. He knew well that sudden death might be waiting for him at the next tree, or even stalking him from behind.

But nothing could frighten him on this night, and he swore a terrible oath: 'Hook or me this time.'

Peter thought about flying but he did not want to give himself away to anyone. So he decided to travel like the redskins. He crawled forward like a snake, leaping up now and again to dart across a clearing on which the moonlight was shining. He dashed along with one finger pressed on his lip and a dagger at the ready. Peter Pan was as happy as could be.

CHAPTER THIRTEEN

The Pirate Ship

One dim, grim light flickered over Kidd's Creek, which is near the mouth of the Pirate River. There lay the brig, the Jolly Roger. She was an evil, dirty-looking ship whose masts and rigging had been repaired with pieces from other ships. The Jolly Roger was a cannibal of the high seas.

The ship was almost silent, except for the sound of the ship's sewing machine at which the hard-working Smee was sitting. A few of the pirates were leaning on the side of the ship drinking rum, and others were playing dice or cards, using rotten barrels for tables. Some pirates, who were sleeping, had taken up positions as far away as possible from Hook's reach, in case he should claw them in passing.

Hook was on the main deck deep in thought. It was his moment of triumph. Peter was dead and all the other boys were on the ship, about to walk the dreaded plank. Yet he was not happy because he was so alone. Hook never felt more alone than when he was with his ragged mob of men. He hated them and they had no great love for him. 'No little children love me either,' he thought.

Hook was not a man to be envied. You could almost feel sorry for him at times.

Hook looked with envy at Smee. Now, there was a man who always thought that every child lived in fear of him. Fear him! Fear Smee! There was not a child on board who did not already love the man. Smee had said horrid things to the children and gently cuffed them with the palm of his hand, because he would not hit with his fist. The children had only liked him more, and Michael had even tried on his spectacles.

Hook would have loved to tell Smee how much the children liked him. But it would be too cruel a thing to do. How could Hook say that to a man who was quite sure he was the most frightening pirate.

Hook's oddly gentle thoughts were interrupted when some of the men started to dance. 'Quiet, you scugs,' he cried, 'or I'll throw the anchor at you. Are all the children chained, so they cannot fly away?'

'Aye, aye,' the pirates replied.

'Then bring them up from below,' said Hook.

All the sad prisoners, except Wendy, were dragged from the dark hold and lined up in front of Hook. 'Now then, me bully boys,' he said. 'Six of you will walk the plank tonight, but I need two cabin boys. Which of you will it be?'

Wendy had told all the boys not to upset Hook, so Tootles stepped forward politely to explain his problem. 'You see, sir, I don't think my mother would like me to be a pirate. Would your mother, Slightly?'

Slightly did not think his mother would like him to be a pirate either. Nor did any of the other boys who stepped forward.

Hook grew angry. 'You, boy,' he said, speaking to John. 'You look as if you have pluck. Did you ever want to be a pirate, my hearty?'

John had indeed. 'I once thought of calling myself Red-handed Jack,' he answered.

'That's a good name, too,' said Hook. 'That's what we'll call you if you join us.'

Michael did not want to be left out. 'What would I be called if I joined?' he asked.

'Blackbeard Joe,' said John, much to Michael's delight. But then Hook told them that they would have to swear 'Down with the King' if they joined. 'Then I refuse,' said John, and Michael said the same.

'Rule Britannia,' squeaked Curly.

Hook's black face turned red with anger. 'That seals your doom. Bring up their mother, get the plank ready.'

They were only young boys and they went white when they saw Jukes and Cecco preparing the plank. But they tried to look brave when Wendy arrived on deck.

No words can describe how Wendy hated those pirates. The boys could at least see some glamour in being a pirate, but all Wendy saw was a ship which hadn't been scrubbed for years. The port holes were so grimy you could scrawl 'Dirty Pig' on every one with your finger. And Wendy had written it several times already.

'So, my beauty,' said Hook. 'You are to see your children walk the plank.'

'Are they all to die?' she asked.

'They are,' he snarled. 'You have time for a few last words with them.'

Wendy told them to be brave. 'Your real mothers would hope that you died like true English gentlemen,' she said.

'We will,' they all cried. Even the pirates were awed by their bravery.

'Tie Wendy to the mast!' cried Hook.

Smee tied Wendy to the mast and when it was done, he whispered: 'I'll save you if you promise to be my mother.' But Wendy replied that she would rather have no children at all.

The boys shivered as Hook, smiling through clenched teeth, took a step towards them. Their time had come.

'Tick! Tick! Tick! Tick! Tick! Tick!'

Everyone heard it, pirates, boys and Wendy. Hook stopped dead in his tracks. He listened in terror for a moment and then fell into a heap, his iron claw lying limply beside him. He began to crawl along the deck, trying to get as far away from the dreaded ticking noise as possible. 'Hide me!' he cried to his men.

They gathered round him, every man's eyes turned away from the terrible creature which was about to come aboard. They did not even think of fighting. If a crocodile was coming, then that was their fate.

Only when Hook was hidden by a circle of pirates did the boys' curiosity lead them to look over the side of the ship to see the crocodile. They got the surprise of their lives. There was no crocodile. It was Peter.

Peter put his finger to his lips to tell them to keep quite. Then he went on ticking.

CHAPTER FOURTEEN
'Hook or Me This Time'

As Peter climbed up the side of the ship, he was thinking how clever he had been. When he left the home under the ground, he had seen the crocodile pass by. It was not until he was in the forest that he suddenly realized that the crocodile had stopped ticking. The clock had finally unwound itself and stopped.

The poor crocodile had lost its tick, its closest friend. Peter decided to put the creature's misfortune to his own use. He started ticking so that the other dangerous creatures of the forest would think he was the crocodile and let him pass safely.

He ticked very well indeed, but there was one unexpected result. The crocodile followed him all the way, probably thinking Peter had stolen its tick. But Peter stayed well ahead of the creature, thinking all the time: 'Hook or me this time'.

He had swum out to the ship and clambered up the side. He was thinking so hard about the battle ahead that he had forgotten to stop ticking. The idea of frightening Hook out of his wits by ticking had not crossed Peter's mind at all. But when he saw the pirates cowering in a corner, he understood what had happened.

He decided at once that, after all, he had thought up the idea. 'How clever of me,' he said to himself, indicating to the boys that it would not be a good idea to burst into applause just then.

It was at this moment that Ed Teynte, the ship's quartermaster, emerged from his cabin and came along the deck. Peter leapt into action, striking true and deep with his dagger. John clapped his hands on the ill-fated pirate's mouth to hide his dying groan. He fell forward and four boys caught him to prevent the thud on the deck. Peter gave the signal and quickly the body was cast overboard.

'That's number one gone,' said Slightly, who had begun to count.

Hook and the pirates heard the splash of the body hitting the water, and, thinking the crocodile had gone, turned around again. The boys were still there but Peter had already tip-toed into a cabin.

'The crocodile has gone,' announced Smee.

'Then I'll raise a cheer to Johnny Plank,' said Hook, raising himself to his full height and breaking into song.

> 'Yo ho, the frisky plank
> You walks along it so,
> Till it goes down and you goes down.
> To Davey Jones below.'

To frighten the boys even more he danced along an imaginary plank. 'Do you want a touch of the cat o' nine tails before you walk the plank?' he smirked.

'No, no,' they all cried. The hideous pirate just smiled and called on Jukes to fetch the dreaded whip. 'It's in the cabin.'

The cabin! Peter was in the cabin! The children stared at each other.

'Aye, aye,' said Jukes and marched into the cabin. The boys watched him go as Hook continued his song:

> 'Yo ho, yo ho, the scratching cat
> In tails of nine, you know,
> and when they are writ upon your back . . . '

What the last line was will never be known because there was a sudden screech from the cabin, followed by a familiar crowing sound. The boys knew whose crow that was.

'What was that?' said Hook.

'Number two,' said Slightly, very solemnly.

The Italian pirate Cecco rushed into the cabin and then came out almost immediately. 'What's the matter with Bill Jukes,

you dog,' hissed Hook, towering over the terrified Cecco.

'The matter with him,' said Cecco, 'is that he's dead, stabbed. But worse still the cabin's as black as a pit, and there is something terrible in there. It's crowing.'

The boys were looking far too cheerful at this stage and Hook saw their mischievous faces. 'Cecco,' he said in his most stately voice, 'go back in that cabin and fetch me that cock-a-doodle-doo.'

Cecco, bravest of the brave, shivered in his boots and cried: 'No! No!'

'Did you say you would not go?' said Hook, stroking his claw.

Cecco went and no sooner had he entered the cabin door than there was another deathly screech and again a crow. Nobody spoke except Slightly. 'Three,' he said.

'Death and odds fish,' thundered Hook. 'Who is to bring me that cock-a-doodle-doo?'

Starkey suggested they should wait for Cecco to come out, but Hook suggested that Starkey might volunteer to go in. 'No, by thunder,' said Starkey.

'By my hook,' said the captain. 'I think you did volunteer because I wouldn't want you to see how playful this hook can be.'

Starkey was determind not to go in and said he would rather swing from the rigging. The other pirates agreed with him completely.

'Is it mutiny, then?' asked Hook, so very politely. 'And Starkey is the ring-leader, is he?'

Every pirate knows that death is the only sentence for mutiny, and Starkey called for mercy. 'Shake hands, Starkey,' said Hook, advancing with his hook all of a twitch.

Starkey looked round for help but none came. He saw the red sparks in Hook's eye and took the only way out. With a despairing shout, he leapt into the sea and vanished.

'Four,' said Slightly.

Hook seized a lantern and swung his claw viciously in the air. 'Now,' he said. 'I'll bring out that cock-a-doodle-doo.' With that he disappeared into the cabin.

'Five.' How Slightly wanted to say the number. It was already on his lips when Hook came out again.

'Something blew my light out,' he said a little nervously. The pirates could see that their captain was not keen to go back into the cabin and talk of mutiny began again.

All pirates are superstitious and Cookson cried: 'They do say that a ship is cursed when there's one more on board than there should be. Is there a stranger on board?'

'Stranger or whatever,' said Mullins. 'Has this something in the cabin got a tail?'

'Has it got a hook?' asked another.

One by one the pirates began to panic and cry: 'The ship is doomed.' At that the children could not resist raising a cheer. Hook had almost forgotten his prisoners, but on looking round a smile lit up his face. 'Lads,' he cried to the crew. 'Here's an idea. Open the cabin door and drive the children in. Let them fight the cock-a-doodle-doo for us. If they kill him, we're so much the better. If he kills them we're none the worse.'

The pirates cheered their captain again and obeyed him instantly. The boys, pretending to struggle, were pushed into the cabin and the door closed.

'Now, let's listen,' said Hook. They all listened but none dared face the door. They turned their backs in fear. In the cabin Peter found the key to the boys' chains and quickly freed them. Then, armed with what weapons they could find, the boys crept out of the cabin.

Peter waved his hand, telling them all to hide, and then flew to the mast and freed Wendy. At that moment nothing could have been easier for them all than to fly away to safety, but one thing stopped Peter; his oath: 'Hook or me this time.'

He whispered to Wendy and she went off to hide with the others while he took her cloak and draped it around himself. Then he stood by the mast, pretending to be her, and took a deep breath and crowed.

The pirates, who still had their backs to the cabin, were panic stricken. Had the unknown creature killed all the boys now? 'Never mind the boys,' whispered Hook. 'I've thought it out. There's a Jonah aboard.'

The pirates all knew what a Jonah was. It was the name they gave to any person who brought bad luck and destruction to a ship. 'Aye,' they said, still feeling in mutinous mood, 'it's probably a man with a hook, and a name the same.'

'No, lads, no,' said Hook. 'It's the girl. A girl always brings bad luck to a pirate's ship. We'll be all right when she's gone.'

The men agreed and Hook told them to fling Wendy overboard. They rushed at the figure by the mast and Mullins cried out: 'no one can save you now!'

'There's one,' came a voice from beneath the cloak.

'Who's that?' said a very puzzled Mullins.

'Peter Pan the avenger,' came the terrible answer. As Peter spoke, he flung off the cloak. Every pirate gasped. So here was the terrible cock-a-doodle-doo.

Hook was speechless for a moment, but then he cried: 'Cleave him to the brisket, lads.'

The children could not imagine what that meant, but when Peter called out, 'Down boys and at them!' they rushed from their hiding places to attack. The pirates were so surprised that they ran in all directions, striking out wildly at anything. Man to man the pirates were stronger, but because they fought while running backwards, the boys could hunt them in pairs and choose which one to attack.

Some of the pirates leapt into the sea and others tried to hide. Slightly ran about with a lamp showing where they were. The pirates were half blinded in the light and quickly fell victim to the other boys' swords.

There was little to be heard except for the clang of weapons, an occasional screech or splash, and Slightly counting '-five-six-seven-eight-nine-ten-eleven.' The last of the pirates were no more when Hook was finally surrounded by a group of the boys. They kept coming closer and closer but all the time he kept them at bay with his swirling hook. One boy who got a little too close was caught by the hook and the captain used him as a shield.

Then another figure, who had just finished off Mullins, sprang into the circle. 'Put up your swords, boys,' cried the newcomer. 'This man is mine.'

Hook found himself face to face with Peter, and the others drew back. The two enemies looked at each other for a long time. Hook shuddered slightly, but there was a smile on Peter's face. 'So, Pan,' said Hook, at last. 'This is all your doing.'

'Aye, James Hook,' Peter answered, 'it is all my doing.'

'Then prepare to meet your doom, my cocky boy,' snarled Hook.

'Have at you,' cried Peter, and the fight began.

Peter was a superb swordsman. He moved so quickly, defending himself against any thrust by Hook with dazzling speed. But the boy was so much smaller than Hook that he could never quite reach the target with his sword.

Hook, not quite so nimble on his feet, was Peter's equal as a swordsman. Yet he was astonished how Peter managed to turn away all his thrusts. The captain began to use his hook as well. It flashed time and time again through the air, nearly slicing the

boy in two. Hook closed in for the kill.

The hook descended once more. But this time Peter doubled up, letting the dreaded weapon racc past above his head. Then he darted forward and pierced Hook in the ribs with his sword.

Hook, you will remember, only feared one thing; the sight of his own blood. When he saw the wound in his ribs he dropped his sword in horror. He was at Peter's mercy. 'Now!' cried all the boys.

But Peter wanted to see fair play. He told Hook to pick up his sword again. Hook did not hesitate, but then he looked at Peter with a very worried eye. Until then Hook had thought he was fighting an ordinary fiend, but now he was beginning to wonder.

'Pan,' he said. 'Who and what are you?'

'I'm youth, I'm happiness,' Peter answered. 'I'm a little bird that has broken out of an egg.'

It was nonsense, of course, but it was proof to the unhappy Hook that Peter did not know who or what he was. 'To swords again,' cried Hook.

Hook now fought with true desperation, his sword sweeping through the air with such violence that it would have cut any man in two. But Peter moved so quickly, darting in now and then to prick his enemy once more in the ribs.

It was too much for Hook. He saw he was beaten and rushed off to the barrel where the pirates kept the gunpowder. Quickly he drew a light and lit a fuse. 'There!' he shouted. 'In two minutes the ship will be blown to bits.'

But it was no use. Peter flew to the barrel and threw the fuse overboard. It was a sign for the other boys to takc to the air. They flew through the rigging and above the decks tormenting Hook with their swords. The captain staggered about, blindly lashing out at the boys who always stayed just out of reach.

Peter advanced on Hook again, cornering him at last. Hook leapt onto the side of the ship, ready to throw himself into the sea. It was the end. Hook knew it. But there was one thing he could still do to save his honour. As Peter flew towards him, Hook cried out: 'Don't waste you sword on me, just kick me into the water.'

That is what Peter did.

It was Hook's final triumph because everyone knows it is unfair to kick someone. 'That was unfair,' cried Hook as he tumbled towards the water.

Of course, Hook did not know that the crocodile was waiting for him below.

The Captain staggered about, blindly lashing out at the boys
who always stayed just out of reach.

So died Captain James Hook.

'Seventeen,' sang out Slightly, but he was not quite correct with his figures. Fifteen pirates died, two escaped to shore. Starkey was captured by the redskins and forced to be a nurse to all their children. Smee escaped too, and he spent the rest of his days saying he was the only man that James Hook had feared.

Wendy took no part in the fight, but now she congratulated everyone. Then she took them into Hook's cabin and pointed to the clock. 'It's half past one,' she said. 'Time for bed.'

She put them all to bed in the pirates' bunks and then went to find Peter. He had been walking up and down the deck until he fell asleep by the Long Tom gun. He had been dreaming and was crying in his sleep. Wendy held him tight.

CHAPTER FIFTEEN

The Return Home

The morning after the fight everyone was up and about early because the pirate ship was rising and falling in a heavy sea. Tootles decided he was going to be bo'sun, the man in charge of the ship's sails and rigging. He set to his new job with enthusiasm, chewing tobacco like every good pirate. In fact they all put on pirates clothes, trousers cut off at the knee and red handkerchiefs for caps.

It does not need to be said who was captain, but Nibs and John were his first and second mate. There was one woman aboard as you might have guessed, but the rest were jolly jack tars, ordinary seamen. They lived in the fo'c'sle at the front of the ship.

Peter had already lashed himself to the wheel like every skipper did in rough weather, and he piped all his crew together to tell them what he expected of them.

'I know you are all pirate scum from the darkest dives of Rio and the Gold Coast,' he barked, as any good captain would. 'But you must do your duty like gallant hearties.'

The crew cheered him loudly as he shouted out a few sharp orders and then they turned the ship around, away from the island, and set a course for the mainland and home.

Captain Pan looked at his charts and calculated that if the good winds lasted, they should reach the Azores about June 21st. After that it would save time to fly.

The crew were a little undecided what sort of ship they wanted. Some wanted it to be a good and honest ship, but others felt they should keep it as a pirate ship. Whatever they thought, Peter was always in charge and had to be obeyed. He treated his men like dogs, just like Hook had, and he demanded instant obedience, just like Hook. Now, what was going on?

The general feeling was that Peter was running a good and honest ship. But was he just pretending so that Wendy would not become suspicious about his real plans? Certainly Wendy did not like it when Peter asked her to make him a new suit out of some of Hook's old clothes. But she did, and when he wore them he seemed to become more like Captain James Hook every day.

At night he would wear the suit in his cabin and smoke two cigars at once with Hook's cigar-holder. Strangely, he would clench one of his hands tightly, leaving just one finger to wriggle free. When he held the hand up against the light of his cabin lamp, an eerie shadow appeared on the wall; it was just like Hook's hook.

*   *   *

But now we must leave Peter and his friends playing pirates to return to No. 14 and the nursery. After all, the children who belong in the nursery are on their way home. We must check that the beds are aired and that Mr and Mrs Darling have not gone out for the evening. Then again, perhaps it would serve the children right if the beds weren't aired and their parents had left for a weekend in the country. Perhaps they need a lesson for leaving home so selfishly.

But, of course, Mrs Darling would not want that. She still loved her thankless children. The beds were aired, and in fact she had not left the house since they had vanished. And the nursery window? Yes, it is open.

Looking through the window we can see that the only change in the nursery rooms is that Nana's kennel is not there. Between the hours of nine o'clock in the morning and six o'clock at night the kennel is never there any more.

When the children flew away, Mr Darling felt he was to blame for what had happened. He was the one who had chained Nana up in the yard. He at last admitted that Nana was perhaps wiser than him. Mr Darling punished himself by getting down on all fours and crawling into the kennel. Mrs Darling tried everything to get him to come out, but he always said: 'No, this is the place for me.'

He swore that he would not come out until his children returned. The once proud Mr Darling was now a very humble man indeed as he sat in the kennel.

Nana often tried to get into the kennel too, but he would not allow it. But he followed Nana's wishes in every other matter.

Every morning Mr Darling got into the kennel. Then it was put into a taxi which took him to his office. He returned the same way at six o'clock. In the past he had always worried what the neighbours thought. Now he held his head high, even when people laughed at him in the kennel. He did not lose his manners either. He would lift his hat politely to any lady who looked inside.

People slowly came to understand why he would not leave the kennel and they felt sorry for him. Crowds followed the cab in the morning, cheering him on. Young girls climbed up to get his autograph. Journalists came to interview him. Rich people asked him to supper, adding: 'Do come in the kennel.'

One Thursday night Mrs Darling was in the nursery waiting for Mr Darling to return from work. Her eyes were filled with sadness. All the happiness of earlier times had vanished because she had lost her children.

As Mrs Darling falls asleep, it would be so nice to whisper in her ear that the children are coming back. They are just two miles away from the window and all are flying strongly. All we need to do is whisper that they are on the way. Let's.

It is a pity we did because we have woken her up. 'O Nana,' said Mrs Darling, to the faithful dog lying beside her. 'I dreamed that the children had come back.' Tears came to Nana's eyes and she put a paw gently on Mrs Darling's lap.

They had not moved when the kennel was brought back. Mr Darling leaned out to kiss his wife. Outside the crowd were still cheering him. 'Listen to them,' he said. 'They are very kind.'

Mrs Darling was beginning to wonder about her husband. He had put himself in the kennel as a punishment, but now could it be that he was enjoying the crowds following him every day? 'Are you sure you are not enjoying it?' she asked.

'My love,' he answered. 'Of course not.'

Mrs Darling said she was sorry for thinking such a thing, but

still believed she was right.

Mr Darling was tired after his day's work in the kennel and curled up like a puppy to go to sleep. 'Play me a tune on the piano to help me sleep,' he said.

Mrs Darling got up and walked towards the piano. It stood in the daytime area of the nursery, away from the beds. 'My dear,' said Mr Darling, 'can you close the window. I feel a draught.'

Mrs Darling was horrified. 'Never ask me to do that,' she said. 'The window must always be left open for them. Always, always.'

It was Mr Darling's turn to apologize as she began to play on the piano. Soon he was asleep.

While he slept Peter Pan and Tinker Bell flew into the room. Where were the children? Surely the plan they discussed on the ship was for Wendy, John and Michael to arrive home first.

Peter's first words tell all. 'Quick, Tink,' he said. 'Close the window. Bar it.'

Tinker Bell did as she was told and Peter continued: 'Good, now we must hide. When Wendy comes she will think her mother has locked her out. She will have to come back with me to Neverland.'

Peter had planned it all along. If he had been pretending to be Captain Hook when they were on the pirate ship, now he was showing all of Hook's cleverness. He did not want to lose Wendy and he was determined that she should return to Neverland.

Peter peeped at Mrs Darling on the piano. 'It's Wendy's mother,' he said to Tink. 'She is a pretty lady, but not as pretty as my mother. Her mouth looks like a thimble, but my mother's looks like many thimbles.'

Of course, Peter knew nothing about his mother, but he always did like to boast about her.

Peter listened to Mrs Darling playing. It was "Home Sweet Home" and, although he did not recognize the tune, he knew it was saying, 'Come Back, Wendy.'

'The window is barred,' said Peter, very pleased with himself as he looked at Mrs Darling. 'You will never see Wendy again.'

Mrs Darling finished playing and Peter saw two large tears in her eyes. 'She wants me to undo the window,' he thought. 'But I won't. Not I.'

He peeped again and saw that the tears were beginning to fall onto her cheek. 'She is very fond of Wendy, I can see that,' thought Peter, getting quite angry. 'I'm fond of her, too.

We can't both have her.'

Peter was irritated and decided not to look at Mrs Darling any more. He skipped about and made funny faces, but somehow he could not get her unhappy face out of his head. It was as if Mrs Darling was inside him, knocking and asking him to let Wendy come home.

'Oh, all right,' he sulked to Tinker Bell, 'we don't want any silly mothers, do we? I'll let Wendy come home if she must.'

With that they unbarred the window and flew out. Just a second later Wendy, John and Michael flew in. They were so pleased the window was open, and never thought for a moment that perhaps they did not deserve to find their way home so easily.

They landed on the floor, quite unashamed at running away from home for so long. Michael had even forgotten this was his home. 'John,' he said, 'I think I have been here before.'

'Of course you have, silly,' said John. 'There is your old bed.'

'So it is!' cried Michael.

'Look!' cried John. 'It's the kennel.' He dashed across to look into it.

'Perhaps Nana is inside,' said Wendy.

But John whistled out aloud. 'Hello? Hello? There's a man inside,' he said.

'It's father!' cried Wendy.

'Let me see,' begged Michael, taking a peep. 'He's not as big as the pirate I killed.'

Wendy and John were puzzled to find their father in the kennel. 'He didn't used to sleep in the kennel,' said John.

'Perhaps we don't remember our old life as well as we thought,' replied Wendy.

It was then that Mrs Darling began to play the piano again. 'It's mother!' cried Wendy, looking at Mrs Darling from behind a bed.

Michael was puzzled now. 'Then, Wendy,' he said, 'you are not really our mother?'

Wendy smiled, realizing that if they had not returned then, Michael would have completely forgotten everything about his old life.

John suggested they should creep in and surprise Mrs Darling by putting their hands over her eyes. Wendy thought they should break the happy news more gently. 'Let's all slip into our beds,' she said, 'and be there when she comes in, just as if we had never been away.'

So when Mrs Darling finished playing and walked back across the nursery, all the beds were fully occupied. The children waited for her cry of joy, but it did not come.

Mrs Darling had seen them, but she could not believe they were there. She saw them in their beds so often in her dreams. Mrs Darling was sure she was still dreaming.

She sat down in the chair by the fire, the place where in the old days she had nursed her children. Wendy was worried and could not understand what was happening.

'Mother!' she cried.

'That's Wendy's voice,' thought Mrs Darling.

'Mother!' said John.

'That's John's,' she thought.

'Mother!' cried Michael. He remembered who she was now.

'And that's Michael's voice,' she thought, dreamily stretching out her arms to hold the three little children. Now what's this? The children had slipped out of bed and now stood right in front of her.

This was no dream. Mrs Darling's arms slipped round Wendy, then John and finally Michael. All three children were back in her arms.

'George! George!' she cried, when she had found her voice again.

Mr Darling awoke to share her delight, and Nana came rushing in too. There could not have been a happier scene, and there was no one to see it; except one strange boy who was staring in at the window.

Poor Peter Pan. He had enjoyed a million adventures in his life, but what he was looking at through the window was one joy which could never be his.

There could not have been a happier scene . . .

CHAPTER SIXTEEN

When Wendy Grew Up

I hope you want to know what happened to the lost boys. They were waiting outside No 14 to give Wendy time to tell her mother about them. When they had counted to five hundred, they went in.

They did not come in by the window. They came up by the stairs, thinking it would make a better impression. Soon they were standing in a row in front of Mrs Darling, with their hats off and rather wishing they were not wearing their pirate clothes.

Not one boy said a word but she could see in their eyes how much they wanted to stay with her. They should have looked at Mr Darling too, but they forgot. Of course Mrs Darling said at once that she would have them, but Mr Darling was very concerned that there were six of them, and that meant six more mouths to feed.

'I must say,' he said to Wendy, 'you don't do things by halves.'

The twins thought he must be talking about them. 'If you think we will be too much of a handful, we can go away,' said the first twin.

'Father!' cried Wendy, shocked.

Mr Darling knew he was being unfair to the boys, but he
could not help it.

'We could always sleep doubled up,' said Nibs.

'George,' said Mrs Darling, sad to see her husband behave so
cruelly. But just then tears came to his eyes. The truth was that
he was as glad as anyone to welcome them. He just thought that
as captain of the Darling house, he should have been asked first
if they could stay.

'We'll find space for all of you in the drawing room,' he
announced.

'We'll all squeeze in,' they promised.

'Then, follow my leader,' he cried happily. 'Mind you, I'm not
sure we have a drawing room. But a sitting room will do.'

The boys danced after Mr Darling and, whether they found
the drawing room or not, I don't know. But they all fitted into
the house somewhere.

As for Peter, he saw Wendy once more that night before he
flew away. He did not exactly come to the window, but he
brushed against it in passing. It was his way of saying she could
open it and talk to him if she wanted. She immediately opened
it.

'Hello, Wendy, good-bye,' he said.

Wendy was sad. 'Are you really going away?' she asked.

'Yes,' said Peter.

Mrs Darling came to the window and told Peter that she was
adopting the boys, and would like to adopt him too. 'Will you
send me to school?' asked the crafty Pan.

'Yes,' said Mrs Darling.

'And then to an office to work?' said Peter.

'I suppose so,' she answered.

'And then I would grow up to be a man?'

'Of course, you would,' she said.

'Ugh!' said Peter, moving a little way from the window.
'I don't want to go to school and I don't want to grow up.
If I woke up one morning with a beard, I don't know what
I would do.'

Wendy said she thought Peter would look lovely with a beard,
and Mrs Darling stretched out her arms to hug Peter.

'Keep back!' he said, rather alarmed. 'No one is going to
catch me and make me a man,' he said.

'But where will you live?' asked Wendy.

Peter explained that he and Tinker Bell would go to live in the
house they built for Wendy on the island. 'The fairies will put it

high up among the tree tops,' he said.

'I thought all the fairies were dead,' said Mrs Darling.

'Oh, no,' said Wendy, who knew a lot about fairies now. 'When a new baby laughs for the first time, a new fairy is born too. So long as there are new babies, there are new fairies.'

Wendy explained how the fairies lived in nests at the tops of trees. 'The mauve fairies are boys,' she said. 'The white ones are girls. The blue ones are silly fairies who don't know what they are.'

'I shall have have such fun,' said Peter, looking at Wendy.

'Won't it be rather lonely in the evening sitting by the fire?' asked Wendy.

'I shall have Tink.'

'You will still be lonely,' said Wendy, just then hearing a rude tinkle of bells from someone hiding around the corner.

Peter saw his chance again. 'If you think I will be lonely, then come back with me.'

Wendy looked at her mother and asked whether she could. 'Certainly not,' she said. 'Now I've got you home again, I mean to keep you.'

'But he does so need a mother,' pleaded Wendy.

'So do you, my love,' said Mrs Darling.

'Oh, all right,' said Peter, pretending that he did not care one way or the other. But Mrs Darling saw something in Peter's eye and knew that he was going to miss Wendy.

She told Peter that Wendy could come and see him for a week every Spring. Then she could do his spring-cleaning. Peter was delighted. He had no sense of time and the thought of Wendy coming to see him every year put a cheeky smile on his face again. He was ready to leave.

'You won't forget me, Peter, will you?' called Wendy as he flew into the sky. 'You won't forget me before spring cleaning time comes, will you? Promise?'

Peter promised as he flew off towards the stars. And do you know what? He took with him Mrs Darling's kiss. It was the one which Wendy and Mr Darling could always see hiding on Mrs Darling's pretty mouth. It was the only kiss they could not get and now Peter was flying off with it. He seemed quite delighted to have got it.

The Darlings watched from the window as Peter vanished into the night sky, his path lit by a bright spark beside him. Peter and Tink had gone.

* * *

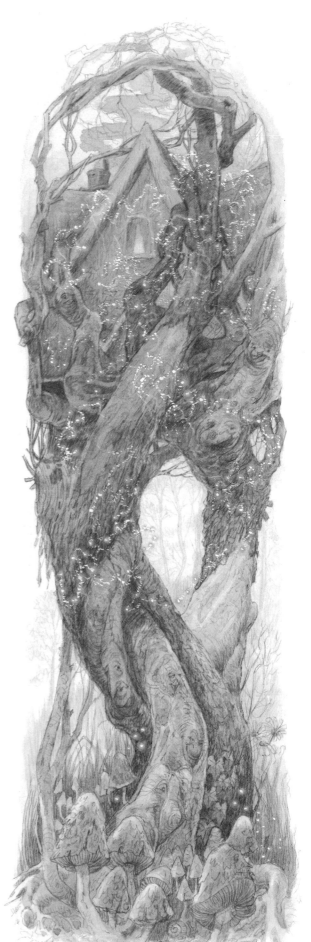

All the boys went to school, Slightly soon finding himself at the bottom of the class. It only took them a week to realize what idiots they had been to leave the delights of the island of Neverland. But it was too late now and they soon settled down to be as ordinary as you or me.

It is sad to say that John and Michael soon lost the power to fly. At first Nana tied their feet to the bedpost at night so they could not fly away. But as time passed they forgot how to fly altogether. They said it was because they did not practice, but the truth was that they no longer believed.

The year passed and Spring came. Peter came for Wendy and they flew away together. She wore the dress she had woven from leaves while she was in Neverland. Her one fear was that Peter might see how short it was. She had grown so much. But he never noticed because he was too busy talking about himself.

Wendy had looked forward to talking to Peter about old times, but new adventures had already filled his head. 'Who is Captain Hook,' he asked when she spoke of his great enemy.

'Don't you remember,' she said, amazed, 'how you killed him to save our lives?'

'I forget them all after I kill them,' said Peter cockily.

When Wendy asked how Tinker Bell was, he could not remember her at all. 'There are so many fairies,' he said. 'I expect she is no more.'

Peter was probably right, for fairies don't live long. But they are so little that a short time seems a long while to them.

Wendy thought how long it had been waiting for Spring to come. Yet to Peter the time seemed to have passed like a short day. But she enjoyed her stay on the island and gave the little house on top of the trees a good spring cleaning.

The next year Peter did not come. She waited in a new dress because she had grown out of the other one. But he never came.

Michael thought Peter might be ill, but Wendy knew he was never really ill. Michael made another suggestion. 'Perhaps there is no such person as Peter Pan,' he said.

Wendy could not believe that, and the next Spring she was pleased when Peter came to see her again. He never knew he had missed a whole year. That was the last time Wendy as a young girl, saw Peter.

Wendy grew up and years came and went without a sign of the forgetful boy. All the boys grew up too. Michael became an engine driver, Slightly married and became a Lord, and Tootles grew a beard and became a judge. And any day of the week you

can see the Twins and Nibs and Curly walking off to the office with their cases and umbrellas.

Wendy got married and had a baby girl called Jane. When she was old enough, Wendy, sitting in the very nursery where this adventure began, told her all the stories about Peter Pan.

It was Jane's nursery now and it held only two beds, one for Jane and the other for her nurse. There was no kennel because Nana had died of old age. At the end she had been very difficult to get on with. She was convinced that no one knew how to look after children better than her.

Once a week, Jane's nurse had the night off and Wendy always put Jane to bed. This was always a time for stories and Jane would raise the bedsheet over her mother's head to make a tent. Then she would whisper: 'We're in Wendy's house, now. What can we see, now?'

'I don't think we can see anything tonight,' Wendy said one night.

'Yes, you do,' said Jane. 'You see the time when you were a little girl.'

'That's a long time ago,' said Wendy. 'How time flies.'

'Does it fly,' asked Jane, 'the way you flew when you were a child?'

Wendy smiled and said she sometimes wondered if she ever did really fly. But Jane was certain Wendy had. 'Why can't you fly now?' she asked.

'Because I'm a grown-up now,' said Wendy. 'When people grow up, they forget. No one can fly when they grow up. You have to be young, innocent and a little selfish to fly.'

Jane wanted to hear the story of Peter Pan again and Wendy told how he had flown in looking for his shadow and how they had all flown off to Neverland. She smiled as she recalled the pirates, the redskins, the mermaids' lagoon, the little house and the home under the ground.

'Which did you like best of all?' asked Jane.

'I think I liked the home under the ground the best,' said Wendy.

'Yes, so do I,' said Jane. 'Tell me what was the last thing that Peter ever said to you.'

Wendy knew exactly what his last words were. 'He said: "Just always be waiting for me, and then some night you will hear me crowing."'

'Is that what he promised?' said Jane.

'Yes,' said Wendy, 'but alas, he forgot all about me.'

A few days later Jane asked Wendy what Peter's crow sounded like. 'It was like this,' said Wendy, trying to imitate the sound.

'No, it wasn't,' said Jane, 'it was like this.' Jane's imitation was much better.

Wendy was a little startled. 'Darling, how do you know?'

Jane said she often heard it when she was sleeping. 'Ah, yes,' said Wendy, 'many girls hear it when they are sleeping, but I was the only one who heard it while I was awake.'

'Lucky you,' said Jane.

And then one night it happened again. It was Springtime and Wendy had just finished telling more stories about Peter Pan. Jane was asleep and Wendy was sitting on the floor by the fire. While she sat she heard a crow. Then the window blew open and Peter dropped down onto the floor.

He was exactly the same as ever. Wendy saw at once that he still had his first teeth. He was a little boy and she was a grown-up. She did not dare move. Somehow it was all so strange now that she was grown up. She was glad it was dark in the nursery so Peter could not see how she had changed.

'Hello, Wendy,' he said, not seeing that she had grown up.

'Hello, Peter,' she answered, something inside her wanting to be a child again. 'Are you expecting me to fly away with you?'

'Of course,' said Peter. 'Have you forgotten it is spring-cleaning time?'

'I can't come,' she said sadly. 'I have forgotten how to fly.'

'I'll soon teach you again,' said Peter.

'Oh, Peter, don't waste the fairy dust on me,' she said. 'I am old, Peter. I am more than twenty. I grew up long ago. Look, I will show you.'

Peter was afraid. 'No, don't turn the light up,' he cried.

But Wendy turned the light up and Peter saw the tall beautiful woman Wendy had become. He let out a cry of pain. 'You promised not to grow up,' he said.

'I couldn't help it,' said Wendy. 'I am a married woman and that little girl in the bed is my baby.'

Peter sat down on the floor and began to cry. Wendy did not know how to comfort him any more and she ran out of the room to think. Peter continued to cry and his sobs finally woke Jane.

She sat up in bed. 'Boy,' she said, 'why are you crying?'

Peter rose and bowed politely to her, and she bowed to him from the bed.

'Hello,' he said.

'Hello,' said Jane.

'My name is Peter Pan,' he told her.

'Yes, I know,' she replied.

'I came back for my mother,' he explained, 'to take her to the Neverland.'

'Yes, I know,' said Jane. 'I have been waiting for you.'

When Wendy returned she found Peter sitting on the bedpost, crowing at the top of his voice, while Jane in her nightie was flying around the room.

'She is my mother,' Peter said to Wendy.

'He does so need a mother,' said Jane.

What could Wendy say. 'Yes, I know,' she finally admitted. 'No one knows it better than me.'

'Good-bye,' said Peter, rising into the air to join Jane.

Wendy rushed to the window. 'No! No!' she cried.

'It is only for spring-cleaning,' said Jane. 'Peter wants me always to do his spring-cleaning every year.'

'If only I could come with you,' sighed Wendy.

'But you can't fly, mummy,' said Jane.

Wendy knew she must let them go and she stood at the window watching them fly away into the sky. She stayed there until Peter and Jane were as small as stars.

*   *   *

All this happened a long time ago and Jane is now an ordinary grown-up too. Wendy's hair has turned grey with age and Jane is married with a daughter called Margaret. Every spring-cleaning time Peter comes to take Margaret to Neverland, at least every time he remembers to.

In Neverland, Margaret tells Peter stories about himself. They are stories which Wendy had told Jane and Jane had told Margaret. They were tales about redskins, ticking crocodiles and an evil pirate called Hook. They were all adventures Peter had long forgotten. But he loved to hear them.

When Margaret grows up, she will probably have a daughter too. That little girl will also be Peter's mother one day. And so it will go on, so long as children still believe in fairies.